MW01242630

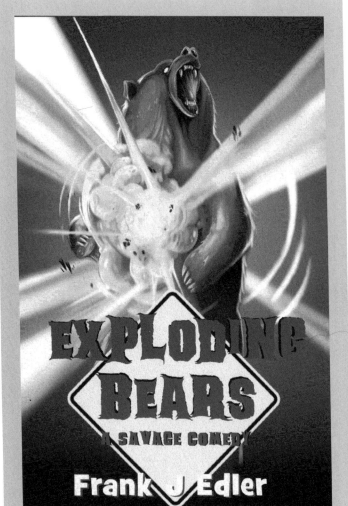

EXPLODING BEARS

A SAVAGE COMEDY

Frank J Edler

Exploding Bears

A Savage Comedy

By Frank J. Edler

This is a work of fiction. Names, characters, businesses, places, events, bears, gifts from the gift shop and incidents are either the products of the author's imagination or used in a fictitious manner. Any resemblance to actual persons (and bears), living or dead, or actual events is purely coincidental. Wearing PPE while reading this book is strongly encouraged.

Cover art by: Stefan Ljumov

Cover Layout by: Frank Edler

Acknowledgements

I'd like to thank the following people who contributed in big and small ways to the creation of this book: Alicia Stamps, editor to the stars. Mort Stone for suffering through this drivel. Armand Rosamilia, Shelly Rosamilia, Chuck Buda, JC Walsh, Nick Zinn, Victoria Nations, Shawna Deresh and AC Ward for writing along side of me at Mando Con while I wrote about blowing up bears. Bud Light Seltzer for obvious reasons. Christina Pfieffer and Marian Elaine for being absolute superstars. And to you, for your morbid curiosity which drove you to pick up this book and find out what a book called Exploding Bears: A Savage Comedy could possibly be about.
Well, you're about to find out.

This book is dedicated to Armand Rosamilia, who blew up a few cows so that I might blow up a metric fuck-ton of bears.

CONTENT WARNING:

EXPLODING BEARS: A SAVAGE COMEDY contains an obscene number of bears that explode, burst, erupt, rupture, fracture or, flat out go *kablooey*. Bears die when they explode, at least, that's what science tells us, so the bears that explode in this book are dead in addition to being exploded. That's all just a part of God's plan.

Occasionally, the bears that explode in this book aren't technically "bears." If
your only problem with bears that explode and die are that they are genuine fuzzy-wuzzy, cute n' cuddly bears, then you'll find momentary moments of comfort when the thing that explodes isn't a bear (in the literal sense) even if someone is telling you it is.

It's okay though, every bear that explodes and dies, even if it isn't truly a cuddly-wuddly, bumbling-fumbling, honey-guzzling bear, in EXPLODING BEARS: A SAVAGE COMEDY, goes to bear heaven (even if it isn't technically a bear) and lives a peaceful and content life forever after.

Also, since this is a "Savage Comedy," whenever a bear explodes, it's funny as fuck.

Carry on.

Chapter 1

Wilson tugged his dad's wrist, leading the way through the mass of people making their way to the observation platform. His targeted spot, a wooden railing that provided a view of the bear enclosure, was in sight. They were at the front of the crowd so, even though his dad was an anchor, slowing him down, Wilson would still get a front-row vantage point to the greatest show on Earth.

"Easy, buddy!" Wilson's dad wasn't as spry as his son, but he did his best to keep up. He wasn't as excited to see the exploding bear but, between the raucous nature of the crowd and the boy's exuberance, his curiosity had peaked in the last few minutes.

A cluster of five fraternity brothers shoved past Wilson and his dad. They hooted and hollered, breaking free of the pack. The meat-headed fivesome were first to the railing. The bros dropped their shorts, revealing targets painted on their asses. Wilson's dad conjured a scene when, earlier in the day, they huddled around each other's asses, painting on the bullseyes.

Wilson and his dad took position next to the frat boys. Wilson climbed up onto the railing to improve his view. The frat guys did the same, only they pointed their ass targets toward the animal enclosure.

Wilson looked at the weirdos, trying to focus on their faces and not the full moons they were shooting. They were daring an animal that wasn't there yet to take aim at their butts. Wilson made a mental note not to be as stupid as they were when he got older.

The crowd filled in along the railing, stacking up five or six deep behind Wilson and his dad. Anticipation grew as the crowd built up. All eyes were peeled on the animal enclosure. It was a semicircle rock wall, bordered by a stand of large pines on either side. The enclosure was separated from the observation platform by a large chasm that prohibited curious wild animals from venturing into the throng of onlookers.

Wilson also thought the chasm was helpful in keeping the onlookers from getting to the animals, given the behavior of the college boys.

A large black bear wandered from behind the trees. It waddled to a bowl of fly-encrusted meat in the center of the enclosure.

The crowd fell into rapt silence. The sudden deadening of noise startled the bear. It stopped and sniffed in the direction of the audience. No doubt the beast could detect all the humans but decided there was no threat. It continued toward its meal.

The bear licked away the mass of flies, revealing the crimson flesh, probably riddled with tiny eggs by that point. Extra protein, the bear would say to itself if bears could think such thoughts. But the bear said nothing, because it was a fucking bear. Instead, it devoured the meat, upsetting the flies' feast.

KA-BLAM!

The black bear exploded, covering the onlookers in charred gore.

One of the college dudes screamed bloody murder.

The others craned their necks to examine his ass.

Wilson caught sight of the bear's muzzle, blown apart from its face, embedded in the guy's butthole. 'Bullseye!' Wilson thought as he felt a numbness in his cheek. He reached his hand up and felt it.

"Fuck yeah, Dad! I got hit with a claw!" Wilson pointed to the black bear's claw impaled in his tender, pink cheek.

"Don't say 'fuck'," Wilson's dad said, wiping away a streak of crimson pooling around the wound.

"Sorry," Wilson said before correcting himself, "I got hit with a shit-cockin' dick-boner of a heckin' bear claw, god damnit."

"That's better son." His dad was careful not to disturb the claw. If it fell out, they'd lose their prize. Why else would you visit Wyld Louie's Exploding Bear Experience? People came from far and wide to witness Wyld Louie's famous exploding bears.

Sea World has Shamu. The whole point of going to see Shamu is to get drenched when the orca belly-flops into his tank. Well, when you went to Wyld Louie's, you expected to be impaled with exploding bear parts. That was the whole reason Wilson raced to the front row of the observation deck.

"Shellac! Resin! Polyurethane, here! Preserve your exploded bear flesh for eternity," a Wyld Louie's

Exploding Bear Experience employee shouted among the crowd.

Wilson's dad stopped the vendor and said, "I'll take a resin. My boy took a claw to the face."

The Wyld Louie's employee examined the wound. "Ahh, yeah. Excellent puncture. A little loose, though. Hang on." The man produced a rubber hammer and tapped the business end against the protruding bear claw. It made a sound like a golf ball being whacked with a graphite club.

"Ow! Fuck! That hurt!" Wilson cried out.

"Language," Wilson's dad reminded him.

"Sorry. That shit-cockin' dick-boner of the rotting ass of my Aunt Tilly's anus hammer hurt!"

"Better."

The vendor gave the tip of the bear claw a wiggle and chuckled. "That baby is lodged in there good, now!"

He worked the upsell by saying, "You're going to want the two-part epoxy for that claw. It'll hold that sucker in there for years, maybe decades. Plus, it really makes the keratin pop."

"Okay, yeah. I'll take the epoxy, sure," Wilson's dad said, spying the name embroidered on the 70s era black satin jacket the employee was wearing. 'Louie' it read in yellow thread script.

"Are you *the* Louie?" Wilson's dad asked as he reached into his pocket for cash to pay the man.

"Wyld Lewuh, that's me," Wyld Louie said.

"Oh," Wilson's dad said, feeling guilty for pronouncing his name wrong. "Lewuh. Sorry, I thought it was Louie."

"Lewuh. That's what I said, Lewuh," Louie said, handing over the epoxy, already moving to make a sale on the dude with the bear muzzle shoved in his ass.

Wilson's dad mixed up the two-part epoxy. Wilson begged his dad to stick around and wait for the next bear explosion. His dad explained that he'd already got what he came for and that they should leave other body parts for kids who hadn't gotten a shattered bear testicle to the face yet.

"Okay," Wilson said, a bit disappointed.

"We can check out the petting zoo," His dad suggested. "You can lick the beaver's ass. They taste just like strawberries!"

"Yeah! Strawberries! Let's go!"

Wilson and his dad moved away from the exploding bear observation deck, making room for the next crowd who were eager to watch a bear go *KA-BOOM*!

Chapter 2

"Jimmuh! We need another exploding bear."

"It's Jimmy, not Jimmuh."

Wyld Louie got pissed. "Why, I ought to eat your ass right here, right now. I said Jimmuh, Jimmuh. Now fetch me a dang bear so I can shove a cracker up its ass the way I'm gonna shove my tongue up your ass."

Jimmy left Wyld Louie's office to fetch a bear for the next (ahem)... demonstration.

Wyld Louie was grumpy. He had to do everything himself if he wanted anything done at all. His name was on the sign out front, he shouldn't have to do shit. But it was hard to find good help. The staff was an unending conga line of idiots, malcontents, derelicts, and disgruntled carnie folk.

There was no way he was going to pay his rabble so much as minimum wage. He'd go broke! Instead, he paid them a flat fee by the day. He told them if they needed more, they had to work the park for tips. That busking spirit gave the park what he liked to call its 'added patina.'

Wyld Louie's Exploding Bear Experience was just that. People came to see a bear explode as if it were some kind of unique species. In reality, Wyld Louie shoved a stick of dynamite up the bear's ass before he sent it out into the enclosure. What people didn't know wouldn't hurt them, and if they knew, fuck 'em anyway.

Any other park would've gone out of business long ago if all they offered was a one trick pony. But the exploding bear experience offered many organic opportunities for added entertainment value.

First, there were the souvenirs. Wyld Louie had opened the joint without a gift shop. He soon realized his paying customers were unhappy leaving without some sort of bumper sticker or t-shirt that said, 'I Saw a Bear Explode at Wyld Louie's and All I Got Was This Crummy T-Shirt.' They do have a gift shop that sells them now though. That's when a genius idea struck Wyld Louie. He ran down to the local home center and bought up all their glue, epoxy, resin and polyurethane. If he didn't have chotskies to sell to people, the bear parts would become souvenirs. Encased in high-gloss epoxy forever and ever, or at least ten to twelve weeks.

Not long after Wyld Louie started on exploding bear souvenirs, one of the employees, Chauncey, brought in his pet hamster and started busking. He claimed it was a dancing hamster. He played 80's dance music like C+C Music Factory and M/A/R/R/S, and he'd set the hamster down on a folding table outside of the exploding bear observation deck.

The hamster didn't dance, it sniffed around for food. Hamsters have a natural charm which draws people to their cute cuddliness. You could advertise a rabid, man-eating hamster and people would still go and pet the dang thing. So Chauncey fabricated a little hand-made sign, claiming his hamster was dancing to Deee-Lite. People were convinced any wiggle and shake the hamster made was dancing and they'd tip Chauncey a dollar or two for the opportunity to pet his little hamster and move on.

"Chaunsuh! That ain't no bear!" Wyld Louie yelled.

Chauncey corrected the pronunciation of his name.

"That's what I said, boy, Chaunsuh! Damnit, boy. I ought to lick your ass right here. Right now. That's insubordination and I'm not gonna tolerate it. Drop your pants, boy!"

Chauncey dropped his pants. He needed the job.

Soon, other employees got in on the animal game and the petting zoo at Wyld Louie's Exploding Bear Experience was born.

There was a snake with a lisp that Larry brought to the petting zoo. "Larruh! I hate snakes, Larruh!" Wyld Louie yelled. Larry got his ass licked.

Barney bought a dingo puppy from a three-toothed man at a roadside exotic animal auction. "Barnuh! That dang dog looks rabid, boy!" Barney received a thorough tongue lashing.

On and on it went until Wyld Louie's tongue was tinted brown and he was forced to put up a square of chain link fence and hang a sign, officially adding a petting zoo to Wyld Louie's repertoire.

Harry brought in the beaver. His boyfriend told him that all the strawberry Yummi-Kakes at the store were flavored with beaver asses because they tasted exactly like strawberries, right before he was locked up at the county jail for seven years. Harry, needing to fill the gap in lost wages, snagged a beaver from the stream out yonder behind their broken down single-wide trailer.

Harry's beaver became the biggest draw to the petting zoo. Folks marveled at the authentic strawberry flavor a beaver's ass provided. Some folks paid twice to get a second lick. Best of all, Wyld Louie said he thought beavers were the second most adorable animal, behind exploded bears.

Jimmy returned with the next bear.

"What the hell is that, Jimmuh?"

"A bear."

"Who ever heard of a black and white bear, Jimmuh? It ain't natural!"

"It's a panda bear, sir."

Wyld Louie was dumbfounded. "Well bend me over and lick my asshole, Jimmuh, that is a genuine panda bear. Do they count?"

"Panda. Bear. Right there in the name, Lewuh... err, Wyld Louie, sir."

Wyld Louie gave Jimmy the stink eye. "Damnit, Jimmuh, you're going to get yourself a severe tongue lashing for that. But later. Right now, I need to load this bear up for the next show."

Wyld Louie opened an old wooden crate sitting in the corner. He retrieved a long red stick of dynamite that would've looked at home in any Roadrunner & Wile E. Coyote cartoon. Louie inspected it for quality, and when satisfied the thing would go KA-BOOM, he walked over to Jimmy and the panda, extended an open hand and said, "Lube me up, Jimmuh."

Jimmy spat into Wyld Louie's hand. Louie's eyes rolled up into the back of his head for a brief, orgasmic moment before he stroked the shaft of the dynamite with the natural lubrication. "Hold on to him good now, Jimmuh. Here we go."

Wyld Louie inserted the dynamite into the panda bear's ass. The panda didn't struggle. It accepted its fate as the exploding bear that it was about to become. Either that or the tranquilizer Jimmy shot him up with made him apathetic to his fate.

Wyld Louie looked at his watch and said, "Showtime, Jimmuh."

Chapter 3

Jenny was used to dealing with the occasional irate customer. Every business has them. No matter how far you went to give your guests a top-notch experience, there was always somebody who claimed they were dissatisfied and demanded a freebie, a discount, or a trip to Tahiti.

Jerry, who made his name abundantly clear to Jenny, time and time again, as if it held some weight, was an irate customer for the ages. He was the type of guest you would remember for a long time to come. Mostly because you dream of thousands of ways you wish you could have or should have murdered him on the spot. Customer service be damned.

"I'm Jerry, damnit!"

"Sir, I understand you're Jerry. You are as important to Wyld Louie as all our other guests. On behalf of the entire staff at Wyld Louie's Exploding Bear Experience, I apologize for your less than satisfactory visit and I'd like to extend complimentary admission to our petting zoo."

"Bullshit! Don't you know who I am? I'm Jerry, for God's sake!"

"Yes, Jerry. I'm aware. Please, I don't normally do this, but I'd also like to extend complimentary tickets for a follow up visit to the Exploding Bear Experience. Perhaps if you give us another try you will find you have a better day."

"Do you know who I am? I'm Jerry! I'd like to speak to your manager!"

"Sir... Jerry, I *am* the manager on duty. I don't wish to have you leave here with a bad experience. What can we do to make this right for you?"

"Well, for one, I'm Jerry. You need to understand that. And two, you can stop all the false advertising."

"False advertising? Sir, I'm not sure I understand."

"Well," Jerry said, glaring at Jenny's name tag, "Jenny, is it? Well, Jenny, what does the sign say out front?"

"It says Wyld Louie's Exploding Bear Experience."

"That's right and I, Jerry, did not see a single bear explode here today."

"With all due respect, sir, a bear exploded during the noon demonstration. It was a sold-out experience. No other guests have complained about the lack of an exploding bear. How is that false advertising?"

"Jenny, I'm Jerry, and I know a bear when I see one and what blew up out there was not a bear!"

"I'm sorry, Jerry..."

"...Jerry."

"Yes, Jerry. Jerry, I assure you it was a bear that exploded at the twelve o'clock noon Exploding Bear Experience. Many of our guests left with exploded bear parts shellacked to their faces. It's a popular souvenir here at the experience. I can offer you a free two-part epoxy kit to remember this precious event."

"I don't have an exploded bear part impaled in me to encapsulate for posterity. Jerry would know if Jerry had a bear part lodged in Jerry's gut!"

"Jerry, you do have a bear part lodged in your gut." Jenny pointed to the black and white tuft of what was once a meaty hindquarter in Jerry's gut.

"Jenny, let me be clear with you. My name is Jerry. You must not know who I am because if you did you would know my name is Jerry. This is not an exploded bear part."

"Jerry, you're confusing me. I can offer you a lifetime of free beaver ass licks for this misunderstanding."

Jerry's poker face broke for a moment. Nobody would ever turn down a lifetime of unlimited beaver ass licks. You'd have to be a fool and Jerry was no fool.

"I'm no fool. I'm Jerry and I will take a lifetime pass for unlimited beaver ass licks, Jenny. But I'm still not satisfied."

"Jerry, that's the trade-off we're going for here. I offer you compensation for your less-than-satisfactory experience and you take the offer in exchange for agreeing that, while a small part of your visit did not meet your expectations, overall, you left with a memorable experience here at Wyld Louie's."

"There's one more thing that you can make right for me, Jenny. Remember my name Jenny, it's Jerry. You can put my name on the marquee out front, right over top of Wyld Louie because I'm gonna own this place with all the money I'm going to rake in for suing you for false advertising!"

Jenny's fuse burned to its end. "Ok. Sir, we're done here. That is a ridiculous demand. Please take your lifetime pass for licking the beaver's ass and leave."

"No! You leave, Jenny! Do you know who I am? I'm Jerry, the new owner of this place!"

All the commotion had drawn the attention of Wyld Louie, who arrived just in time to hear Jerry declare himself the new owner of Wyld Louie's Exploding Bear Experience.

"Just what in the hell is going on here, Jennuh?" Wyld Louie demanded.

Before Jenny could answer, Jerry cut in, "Do you know who I am?"

"You're Jerruh."

"Jerry."

"That's what I said, Jerruh."

"No. You're saying Jerruh, not Jerry. My name is Jerry."

"Damnit, Jerruh!" I won't have guests disrespecting me. You go on and get out of here before I drop your pants and lick your ass like your mama should've done to you years ago!"

"My mother named me Jerry so the world would know who I am! Do you know who I am? I'm Jerry, not Jerruh, for crying out loud!"

"That's it!" Louie keyed the mic on the walkie-talkie he had clipped to his belt and yelled, "Securituh! Securituh! We've got a situation."

At a moment's notice, Jimmy and Chauncey showed up. Both of Wyld Louie's security detail detained Jerry by the arms.

"Damnit, you let go of me!" Jerry said to the Wyld Louie's Exploding Bear Experience security team. "Don't you know who I am?"

Before Jerry could tell security who he was, Wyld Louie did the explaining for him, "This is Jerruh."

"Jerry."

Wyld Louie grunted, "Jerruh here will be getting an ass licking before the two of you escort him off the premises."

Jimmy and Chauncey nodded. Wyld Louie maneuvered behind Jerry. Jerry looked nervously over his shoulder. He let out a whimper when Wyld Louie tugged down his trousers in one, swift motion.

Wow, Jerry was impressed and mortified at the efficiency in which Wyld Louie was able to depants him. That guy must be a professional. And then, Jerry felt a sensation on his bottom that made him forget his own name for a few minutes.

Jenny looked on and sighed. When was Wyld Louie ever gonna lick her ass?

Chapter 4

Wyld Louie fidgeted with a stick of dynamite like it was a cheap toy. He called Jimmy for the next bear. Jimmy didn't protest on the pronunciation of his name, instead he went to retrieve another bear for the next exhibition.

A giant, white ursine animal slunk into the room.

"Good God! What in the hell is that, Jimmuh?"

"Polar bear, sir."

"Christ-on-a-crapper, Jimmuh! You have to warn me when you're going to bring in a big one. You nearly scared the ass of off me."

The polar bear laid down and took a nap.

"Damnit, Jimmuh, how much dope did you dope this dopey bear with?"

"I gave him three. He's pretty big."

"He? I thought all polar bears were of the female variety?"

"I mean, I'm pretty sure I saw a big ole ding-a-ling swinging true between his legs."

Wyld Louie moved to the bear's hindquarters. He gave the bear a shove to get it on its side so he could spy this supposed, impressive bear junk. The hulking beast didn't budge despite Louie's efforts.

Jimmy offered to help roll the snoozing bear on its side. The two men could not get the beast to roll. Wyld Louie, not to be deterred, reached under the bear to probe for its alleged phallus.

As the two men were shoulder deep in their search for the elusive polar bear penis, Jenny arrived and asked, "Is everything okay?"

Wyld Louie called out around a mouthful of white polar bear fur, "Damnit, Jennuh, we're looking for this dang bear's dong. Get in here, would you? You must be good at finding polar bear schlongs, being as you're a lady."

"Wyld Louie, bears don't have penises. You'll be hard pressed to find one."

"Damnit, Jimmuh! I told you all polar bears were ladies!"

"There was something swinging between this bear's crotch before! I swear to it!"

"Beans n' rice, Jimmuh! If this bear turns out to have a vajang, I swear, I'll be licking your ass from here to Friday!"

Jenny flashed green with jealousy at another threat of ass licking not aimed at her. What the hell was wrong with her? Wyld Louie licked everybody's ass but hers. This was bullshit!

"This is bullshit!" Jenny said before stomping out. She neglected to explain that the male polar bear didn't have a penis, but it sure had a bacula, or penis bone, which gave polar bears the rod they were looking for. Fuck 'em.

Wyld Louie and Jimmy looked at each other, confused about Jenny's sudden mood swing. Women were such odd creatures. Bears were less complicated.

"Come on, Jimmuh," Wyld Louie said, calling off the search for the bear's dick like it was a person lost at sea for too long, "we'll find the dong after we blow up this polar bear. Something that big is bound to get lodged in some poor chap's abdomen."

Wyld Louie loaded the stick of dynamite into the polar bear and Jimmy coaxed the lethargic bear out onto the exhibition stage.

The crowd cheered when they saw they were about to be treated to a polar bear explosion.

The bear waddled over to a pile of meat at the center of the enclosure. Before it could take a whiff of the rancid pile of meat...

...*KA-BLAM*!

Wyld Louie was out in the crowd with his cart of epoxies, shellacs and spray glue faster than pieces of bear could project at sonic speeds into the crowd.

"Shellacs! Two-Part Epoxies! Polyurethane! Save the memories of an exploding bear for a lifetime! Anyone got a big ole bear dong lodged in them?"

Wyld Louie wandered back and forth through the crowd. He found someone who may have had a testicle impaled in their shin, but it could have been an eyeball. Another patron had a wad of white goop matted in their hair. It could've been a wad of bear jizz, or it could've been a liquified titty sac. Nothing that looked like the remains of a hairy, white penis.

Fucking Jimmuh was in for a right-stern ass licking. That dang bear was a girl just like he said to begin with.

"Have you seen Jimmuh?" Wyld Louie asked a random guest with a long, thin bone protruding from his forehead. Wyld Louie cursed the stunned guest, who had a polar bear penis bone tickling the edge of his brain and went to find Jimmy.

Chapter 5

"This line is ridiculous," Wilson's dad said.

"Hey, Dad, has my claw dried yet?" Wilson started to touch the tip of the bear claw to answer his own question.

His dad swatted Wilson's finger away before he could touch the tip of the claw, impaled into his son's cheek. "Don't touch it. That epoxy still needs another five hours to set."

"Ugh! It's gonna take forever!"

"You wanted to keep the bear claw, didn't you?"

"Yeah, but I didn't know it was going to take forever. I don't want it in my cheek anymore, Dad," Wilson whined.

The sun had reached its precipice. The heat wore on the father's patience and his son's sanity. Waiting in line to lick the beaver's ass wasn't helping. It wouldn't have been that bad if it weren't for the oppressing heat.

His dad knelt down to Wilson's eye level. "Why don't we go over and watch the dancing hamster show? By the time it's over, maybe the beaver line will be much shorter. What do you say, sport?"

"I don't wanna watch a dancing hamster. That's stupid. I wanna lick the fucking beaver's ass."

"Language," Wilson's dad reminded him.

"Sorry. I wanna lick the shitass-eating, twat-boot licking, asshole-flinging, booger-chewing beaver's ass," Wilson said, correcting himself and then added, "you god damned sonovabitch."

"Better," his dad said, but they still needed to get the heck out of the beaver ass licking line. "Hey, look! Over there... We can pet a broken-fanged rattlesnake. That sounds pretty cool, right? And safe?"

"Dad, I wanna lick the beaver's ass and see if it really tastes like strawberries."

His dad sighed. He stood up and scanned the petting zoo's other offerings, hoping to spot something that would grab his son's imagination more than a beaver's ass. There was a flea-infested spider monkey. 'Pet two different animals at once,' the sign exclaimed. There was a donkey still dripping with a fresh coat of purple spray paint. One sign caught the father's attention, 'Poke a finger in the llama toe!'

"Wilson, they've got a llama."

"That's an alpaca, Dad," Wilson said, staying laser focused on the line in front of them.

"Well, maybe alpaca asses taste like snozzberries," his dad said, frustrated.

Wilson's nose wrinkled and he said, "Snozzberries? Who ever heard of snozzberries?"

His dad said, "We are the music makers and are the dreamers of dreams."

Wilson shrugged.

He decided his son needed to watch the classics.

He was fed up. It was time he pulled rank. "Wilson, I'm not waiting in this line any longer just to lick a beaver's ass. C'mon, it's time to go."

"No!" Wilson stomped. He drew a line in the sand and drew the attention of everyone waiting in line.

His dad surveyed the faces of those around him. Nobody was sympathetic to his suffering. They were all on Team Beaver's Ass.

"Fine. Fine," his dad conceded, more to everyone else in line than to his son. "We'll wait for the beaver's ass."

The line moved forward a step. "See, Dad. The line is moving now!"

His father grew frustrated. The line moved one step forward, big deal. That would get Wilson's hopes up for about thirty seconds before he grew impatient again and started whining. It wasn't the line that he hated, it was his son's pissing and moaning that grated on his nerves, he needed a distraction too.

As luck would have it, a representative of Wyld Louie's Petting Zoo worked his way along the line, cradling a tiny little gerbil with the biggest black marble eyes you ever did see. Wilson's dad was so smitten with the adorable creature, he couldn't resist letting out an audible, "Aww!" when he saw the little fucker.

The gerbil wrangler, who was working the beaver ass licking line for tips, proffered the gerbil to Wilson's dad. "Wanna pet him?"

"Oh yeah!" He said.

Without hesitation, he stroked his finger along the gerbil from head to tail and repeated the motion in a near frenzy. He slowed his pace after a few therapeutic strokes.

His heart rate had settled to normal levels. "He's so cute."

The gerbil wrangler made his pitch, hoping to get the man to choke up some cold hard cash. "He's got the gout."

The father's heart poured out for the poor animal. Out of a sense of genuine compassion for the wee creature's suffering, he kissed it and hoped a small dose of love would help it heal.

"And he's got syphilis, too."

The dad froze. Syphilis. Great.

He reached into his pocket and tipped the gerbil wrangler a dollar.

"Thanks, mister. I'll be sure to get him a penicillin shot soon!"

The gerbil wrangler moved along up the line. The father wiped his lips with the back of his arm.

Fuck.

Chapter 6

KA-BLAM! Another polar bear exploded.

Wyld Louie had loaded the son-of-a-bitch with a few extra sticks of TNT. He was a big boy (dammit Jimmuh, he better have been a boy) and Louie wanted to be sure he gave it the right amount of bang. The guests would turn on him in a heartbeat if he provided a less-than-spectacular exploding bear.

Claws, eyeballs, teeth and tails blasted the crowd like chunks of watermelon at a Gallagher show. The overload of dynamite cooked hunks of polar bear meat like steaks on the grill. Hot slabs of juicy polar bear meat rained upon the assembled.

A kid bent down and picked up a steaming chunk of bear and put it in his mouth.

"Don't eat that!" his father admonished, "you don't know where it's been!"

The boy talked around a mouthful of polar bear meat, "I know where it's been, we just watched it blow up."

"That landed on the ground. It's got germs!" the father reminded the kid.

"Dad, you said cooking the meat kills germs."

The father was stymied by his own kid's logic. "How long was in on the ground?"

"Like, four seconds."

"And you kissed it to God before putting it in your mouth?"

"Just like you taught me."

His father shrugged, leaned down and snagged his own piece of charred polar bear meat. He held it to the sky for God to see and placed a kiss on the roast. He tore into it like a damned carnivore and savored the umami flavor of a perfectly cooked piece of beef.

Beef? No, that was a cow. What did you call bear meat, anyway? Pig was pork. Chicken was poultry. Deer were venison. As the man chewed on the juicy piece of bear meat, he reached into his pocket and withdrew his cell phone. He googled "What is bear meat called?"

Bear meat is called bear meat, Google informed him. That was lame. The man decided that bear meat needed an awesome moniker like beef or pork or mutton. Bork. That was it. Bork!

"This is great bork!" He exalted.

The urgency of FOMO rushed through the assembly. Guests searched the ground for their own chunks of bork. In moments, the crowd on the exploding bear observation deck turned into a pack of sharks in a feeding frenzy.

The excitement drew the attention of Wyld Louie as he made his way onto the platform to hock his various adhesives. He was terrified to find his guests shoveling hunks of charred bear meat into their maws. No! If they filled up on bear, they wouldn't be hungry, and Wyld Louie's Wyld Café and Toilets would be empty.

"Hey! Hey!" Wyld Louie grabbed chunks of bear tenderloin and bear steaks and bear drumsticks out of his guest's hands as they fed. "That's my bear meat! You have to pay for that!"

"It's not meat, it's *bork*!" the discoverer of bork shouted in Wyld Louie's face, grabbing back his chunk of bork.

"Whatever it is, you can't have it here. Food is only to be consumed in the Wyld Louie's Wyld Café and Toilets! That's the policy around here. No outside food or beverages."

"This ain't outside food or beverage. This is bork from the exploded bear. It's a by-product!"

"Bullshit! It's product, and you need to pay for it! Five dollars a hunk! No exceptions. No freebies!"

The bork discoverer took another bite out of his hunk of bork in defiance. "I ain't paying."

Wyld Louie got on the radio and said, "Securituh! We've got a situation on the deck. Jimmuh! Chauncuh!

Barnuh! Larruh! All hands to the observation deck, now!"

The man and all the others around him ate bork while waiting for security to arrive. By the time Jimmy, Chauncey, Barney and Larry got to the observation deck, everyone was finished eating.

"Jimmuh, escort this gentleman and his party off the premises. He's stealing from me!"

"Stealing what, sir?"

"Bear meat!"

"Bork," the bork man corrected.

"He's eating the bear meat, Jimmuh! He's stealing all my profits."

"Sir, we don't sell bear meat," Jimmy said.

"Bork." The bork guy was getting agitated.

"Damnit! Jimmuh, I should lick your ass and charge you double for it! Don't correct me! From now on, we charge for bear meat." Wyld Louie looked to his left. Larry was the first person in his sights. "Larruh, from now on you're on bear meat duty. You collect up all the good pieces and bring them to the cafe. No eating or drinking during the demonstrations. You hear me?"

"I hear you, Wyld Louie, sir. But, it's Larry, not Larruh."

"That's it! Jimmuh, get this freeloader out of here. I've got to teach Larruh a damned lesson."

Chapter 7

Jenny had one job at Wyld Louie's Exploding Bear Experience: do whatever Wyld Louie asked her to do. Her job was the same as everyone else's job. There wasn't much in the way of job descriptions, employee handbooks or standard operating procedures when you went to work for Wyld Louie. You showed up, did what Wyld Louie asked of you, and hopefully got paid.

Despite the fact that, in theoretical terms, she was supposed to have been working on equal terms with her co-workers, Jenny found that she always got the short end of the stick.

Jimmy got to wrangle the bears. Jenny never did.

On top of his dancing hamster gig, Chauncey managed the petting zoo, which Jenny never got to do.

Larry picked up animal crap and had the snake gig. Not Jenny.

Barney cleaned up the human crapper and had his dingo. Jenny got to sit in the office and do none of it.

Jenny was customer relations. The ticket and money girl. She rarely ever left the office. She had the cutest little parakeet at home. She named him Nut because he had elephantiasis in one of his testicles. Normally, avian testicles are located inside the body of the bird, but Nut's nut was so big it had prolapsed outside of his body. Nut's testicle was about the size of a grape, which doesn't sound that big until you considered that Nut was only about five inches tall. His big, grey ball looked like a tumorous growth on his abdomen, but if you rubbed it the right way, Nut would nut all over your hand like a tiny little Ron Jeremy with wings.

Nut was able to fly. The weight of his nut kept him Earth-bound. But he was adorable. And he loved people. He loved to perch on a finger and have his head, or his nut, petted. He would've been the perfect addition to Wyld Louie's Petting Zoo. They lacked a bird in their arsenal. Nut would have filled in the gap.

But Wyld Louie would always say, "Damnit, Jennuh, you can't bring a bird to the petting zoo. How are you supposed to take care of the bird *and* collect money at the same time?"

So Jenny missed out on collecting tips to pad her income.

There was something else Jenny always missed out on: having her ass licked for bad behavior.

If Jimmy wrangled a sick bear that wouldn't 'perform', he'd get his ass licked.

If Chauncey corrected Wyld Louie about anything he said, or the way he said it, he got a tongue lashing to his rear.

When Larry failed to clean out the overloaded crapper and paying guests left before they could stop at the gift shop, Wyld Louie had him bent over, reciting the Pledge of Allegiance while his bung hole got reamed.

And Barney? It seemed all Barney had to do was look at Wyld Louie the wrong way and Wyld Louie wrestled him to the ground, yanked his pants around his knees (if Wyld Louie was even patient enough to take the time to get them down to his knees) and had a somewhat voluntary two-man human centipede made of him. Heck, Barney even got to shit in Wyld Louie's mouth once.

But Jenny? She could give out discount tickets without a coupon and her posterior would remain drier than the Sahara. She could correct Wyld Louie about the way he said her name until the cows came home and the only stink he would make would be a stink eye in her direction. Once, she didn't show up for work, didn't even call in, and the only tongue lashing she received from Wyld Louie was a verbal one.

What did she have to do to get punished like the others? She hated being the only girl at the all-boys club. It wasn't fair.

If Wyld Louie didn't see the unequal treatment, at least Jimmy did.

"He'll lick your ass one day. I'm sure of it, Jenny. He's probably just waiting for it to be... special."

Special. Jenny liked the sound of that. If Wyld Louie ever did chow down on her ass like it was the midnight special at the all-you-can-eat buffet for starving children in China, it was going to be special.

Jimmy always planted a seed of hope in her un-tongued asshole. He was right. When Wyld Louie handed out severe tongue lashings, it was a dime-a-dozen act. There was nothing meaningful about it. He only did it to encourage proper behavior. He was a father teaching his kids a lesson.

But, when he finally got to Jenny (oh, she hoped beyond hope Wyld Louie would finally get to her) it would be a different thing altogether. It would be like fucking your husband who's a porn star in those 6-hour porn DVDs. You know the type, there's like one hundred sixty-seven vignette scenes and he's in eighty-three of them, and in the course of five minutes, twelve scenes out of those eighty-three, he takes it in the ass as much as he gives it in the ass. But, after that filthy, unadulterated, syphilis infused, triple-dose of penicillin afterwards fuck fest, he still goes home to his wife and makes beautiful love to her all night long.

Jenny wanted to be that porn star's wife with Wyld Louie. He was going to lick her ass like God had intended asses to be licked, with tenderness, understanding and devotion.

The thing was, she'd waited this long. She couldn't wait any longer.

"Well, tonight's going to be the night. I'm done waiting," she told Jimmy.

Jimmy was curious and asked, "How do you know that?"

Jenny crossed her arms over her chest and said, "Because I'm going to make it happen. And you're going to help."

Jimmy's eyes went bigger than an exploded bear's asshole. "What? Me, help? No. No way. He'll just get pissed at me for conspiring against him and lick my ass instead of yours. No thank you. You're on your own."

"No, Jimmy. You're not going to be there. You're going to help me set the mood."

Color Jimmy intrigued, he wanted to hear more about Jenny's plan. They had a few minutes while Wyld Louie was off shilling his latest trinket in the gift shop: an exploding bear snow globe. It was made of cheap plastic and filled with water likely sourced from irradiated ponds in Chernobyl. Within that fluid floated cheap, plastic bear parts. It contained four legs, a torso, a head and, of course, a little red heart that made it so cute, every little girl who passed through the gift shop just had to have one.

"Okay, so during the next demonstration, when he's distracted again, this'll be what you need to do..."

Jenny laid out her plan for an evening of deep, meaningful ass licking between two consenting adults.

Chapter 8

Wilson was so excited that he was doing the pee-pee dance. "We're almost there, Dad!"

They had made it to the point in the line where nothing separated them from beaver ass glory. "Yup, we're next, buddy. Do you need to go to the bathroom?"

Wilson tittered back and forth on his two legs and absentmindedly had a hold of his little boy dong with one hand. "No. I'm good. I mean, I do gotta go, but I can hold it."

"You sure? I don't want any accidents."

Wilson responded by gripping harder on his unit. The need to pee rushed to his nether regions when they made it to the head of the line. Wild anticipation always made him want to piss like an overstimulated puppy. It was the type of excitement only children felt. As you grew older, a kind of disappointed patience shoved down childlike eagerness, fueled by unyielding bouts of disappointment that went hand in hand with adulting.

His dad knew it. That's why he didn't push for the bathroom. Not that they would've stepped out of line at this point to run to a urinal anyway. They'd waited too long and come too close to glory to bail out now. If it really got that bad, he'd just let Wilson run over to the bushes and relieve himself while he held their place in line.

He figured the humanity in everyone else waiting would cause them to understand and give them a pass on holding things up.

But it never came to that. Wilson and his dad watched as the group in front of them took turns having a go at the beaver's ass like it was a Tootsie Pop. They were taking turns researching the age-old question, 'How many licks *does* it take to get to the center?'

Before long the group did what needed to be done and moved along.

Harry, the beaver handler, waved Wilson and his dad into the beaver licking area.

The beaver sat on a high wooden table. The beaver was sitting calmly on a cushion which had a cut out in the rear to provide unobstructed access to the beaver's ass end. Harry had one hand on the beaver's back, which calmed it and held it in place. Not that the beaver was jumpy about having its ass licked.

In fact, Wilson's dad had been observing the beaver's demeanor as the others in front of them took their turn. In his estimation, the varmint was really into getting its bum licked. The rodent never flinched or cringed. If anything, Wilson's dad would swear he saw it quiver at the touch of a few of the tongues.

Wilson ran up to the beaver the same way Indiana Jones approached a talisman, with enraptured caution.

Harry nodded to Wilson to have his lick. Wilson closed his eyes tight. He stuck out his tongue like he was waiting for a snowflake to fall on it. He hesitated, the only other time in Wilson's life he would experience this much nervous anticipation will be when he kisses Jenny Lee Lumburger for the first time. But that will be years away and this is now. When Wilson finally did connect his tongue to that beaver's ass, the rush the beaver felt will be the same rush Jenny Lee feels years later.

His dad placed his hand on Wilson's shoulder and asked, "How's it taste?"

Wilson pulled away from the beaver's ass. He smacked his lips a few times, examining the flavor the way a wine connoisseur contemplates the flavor notes in a sip of Merlot. "It tastes like..."

"...strawberries?" his dad asked.

"No. Like," Wilson smacked his tongue to the roof of his mouth again, opening up the bouquet, "like, beef stew."

"Beef stew?" His dad didn't like the way that sounded.

"Yeah, like when grandma used to make it. I taste the boiled carrots, potatoes and earthy meat. The thick, brown gravy too!"

Wilson was excited about the flavor. His dad was repulsed. Beaver asses were supposed to taste like strawberries, not beef stew. Someone who doesn't wipe their ass very well has an ass that tastes like beef stew.

Wilson's dad looked at Harry. "What the fuck?"

Harry shrugged. He looked nervous.

The father took a look at the beaver's ass. He wasn't sure what beaver asses should look like, but he did have an idea of what a beaver's pelt should look like and this beaver had an odd-looking pelt.

The hair was thick and stiff, more like reeds of straw than fur. His dad took a gander at the supposed beaver's mouth. Beavers were supposed to have big, bucked teeth to gnaw through trees so they could damn up rivers and stuff with them. This particular beaver flashed no impressive incisors. Plus, its snout looked a bit more elongated than what he recalled a beaver's face should look like.

"Are you sure this is a beaver?" Wilson's dad asked like a pulp detective.

Harry shifted himself between the dad and the beaver. "Yeah, I know a beaver when I see one." He looked at Wilson and said, "Tastes just like strawberries, right?"

Wilson beamed. "Not really. But it does taste just like grandma's beef stew!"

The next few patrons in line heard Wilson's declaration. A murmur grew through the line. Was there tomfoolery afoot?

"Beaver ass is supposed to taste like strawberries, not stew. What's going on here? This ain't no beaver." Sherlock-dad announced his presumption and laid out his accusation.

"Sir, this is a genuine, North American Dam Beaver." Harry tried to assure the dad as well as the rest of the crowd, who had questions about the authenticity of the beaver experience they'd waited in line for.

"Dam beaver, you say?" Wilson's dad said, pulling out his phone and navigating to the Google search bar.

Harry's eyes shifted around. "Yes. It's a local breed. May not be on the internet yet."

The father ceased his Google search, knowing there was no North American Dam Beaver to be found. "I want my money back. My son says your beaver's ass tastes like beef stew, not strawberries. I demand satisfaction."

"No refunds," Harry said defiantly.

"What kind of animal is this? Really?" Wilson's dad asked, pressing the matter further.

"North American Dam Beaver."

"That's not a real thing. Is this a sick racoon?"

Harry scoffed. "That ain't no racoon."

"Woodchuck."

"*Pfft*. Woodchucks are way fatter than this porcup..." Harry stopped himself. He had let the truth slip.

"Porcupine?" This is a porcupine? You just let my son lick a porcupine's ass?!"

"I shaved it," Harry offered, as if it were an OSHA approved concession.

"My son could've lost an eye! He could have been poisoned! I want my money back. Now. And, you can believe I want to talk to your manager."

Wilson was getting nervous. His dad was super upset, and he didn't know why. The beaver's ass tasted pretty good, even if it wasn't strawberries. Now his dad and the animal guy were yelling about porcupines and acting as if Wilson were going to die. It escalated beyond his ability to follow the adult argument. Wilson just wanted to go pet the legless snake now.

"No refunds," Harry repeated.

"Fine. Then you're going to find me a beaver. Right now. And you're going to let my son lick its fresh, just picked, first harvest, wild, organic, strawberry flavored ass. And you're going to do it for free."

Harry giggled. "Who's gonna make me?" he asked, sizing up the father.

Wilson's dad was scrawny and he knew it. He had been a bean pole his entire life. Lanky, no musculature, emaciated, even. Being a dad sometimes made him braver than he was when it came to protecting his son. The beaver kid was in his twenties and pretty fit. Buff, even. He knew he didn't have a chance in a physical confrontation. He didn't know how he would make the guy capitulate to his demands.

The next guest in line for beaver ass licking stepped up and said, "I'm gonna make you."

The dad looked over his shoulder. His rescuer was massive. He had biceps like whisky barrels. The man's chest was as big across as a queen-sized mattress. He wore denim overalls and was shirtless. Wilson's dad noted his bald head and thick, über-manly beard. It grew on his face like a well-kept Chia Pet.

To the dad, he looked like an angel.

The guy put a massive, reassuring hand on his shoulder and said, "Hey. I'm Angel." Then he looked at Harry again and said, "You're gonna get this nice gentleman and his son a genuine beaver's ass to lick. And then my son is gonna lick the beaver's ass. And then, if you do a good enough job, I might let you lick the beaver's ass so you don't make this terrible mistake again."

Chapter 9

"Damnit, Jimmuh! I said no more of these black ones. There's nothing vicious about them."

Jimmy sighed. Wyld Louie never concerned himself with *how* he obtained bears to blow up, just as long as he got them. He wished Wyld Louie could appreciate the myriad tactics Jimmy utilized to find six bears a day, every day: five days a week. If Wyld Louie had to do these things himself, he might appreciate the work Jimmy put in and understand the obstacles he had to navigate in order to procure a bear for each demonstration. There might be a whole lot less ass licking going on if that were the case.

Black bears were the easiest. Jimmy could go out into the woods around Wyld Louie's Exploding Bear Experience and pick them off all day long. They were maggoty in the forest. Black bears were the most common bear around. Jimmy didn't even have to trap them. He just put out a basket full of cookies or cakes or pre-packaged bakery pies (they loved the chocolate pudding filled pies best) and the bears would flock to the feast. They'd follow Jimmy straight back to Wyld Louie's, where he'd tranq them and get them out in time for the show.

But Wyld Louie hated them because of YouTube. YouTube was ruining the fabric of the American experience. And it all started with videos of black bears being all cute and fuzzy and cuddly at drive-thru safaris across America.

The drive-thru safari businesses loved black bears. They were large and imposing, but they were also docile, even skittish. They didn't pose a serious threat to humans, even though the gut reaction people have toward them is to run, screaming in terror.

That fact was exposed like a festering, oozing wound on the collective consciousness of Americans in the form of YouTube videos. Go on, search 'black bear' on YouTube and you'll be met with a barrage of video after video of black bears doing things normally reserved for the cutest of mammals, the otter. Black bears waved at cars passing by as if they were old man Johnson, sitting on his front porch in his rocking chair, sipping on his lemonade and waiting for a car to roll past so he could do his favorite thing in the whole world, wave at it. Black bears would roll around on their backs in the gravel like an over-excited puppy getting at an itch he couldn't easily reach with his paws. There's even video of black bears snuggling up with other cute animals like cats or goats or lions or hyenas. Adorable.

Wyld Louie hated them. His guests were always less than enthused when they saw a black bear prance out into the demonstration enclosure. There would always be that collective, 'Awwww' when they recognized the cute black bear and then realization settled in that they were about to witness this adorable animal explode and rain down bloody hell upon them.

That's when Wyld Louie would have to work the crowd, selling his epoxies and adhesives, assuring the guests that it wasn't a black bear but one of his genuine exploding bears. People were dumb. They believed there was a species of bear that exploded like they were some sort of bombardier beetle.

"Don't have time to get another before showtime," Jimmy reminded Louie, "he's gonna have to do."

Jimmy would love to see what Wyld Louie would do if he ever took a sick day or, God forbid, up and quit. Then how would he get bears? Sometimes, Jimmy would daydream about that very scenario. He pictured Wyld Louie out there in the forest, stalking bears, only finding black bears and getting frustrated. Wyld Louie would probably spend hours hunting his favorites, grizzlies and polar bears. Jimmy would've bet good money that Wyld Louie didn't know that polar bears and grizzlies don't live in the woods around here.

Jimmy, of course, had other ways to source bears. He had honed his techniques over time. The woods were always a last resort for him when other channels dried up. Like, you never really knew how many roadside zoos there were across this great land of ours until you happen across a periodical that catered to advertising orphaned animals that came from all these tiny zoos. Invariably, they all close down because the owners have no clue how to run a roadside zoo. But Jimmy was fortunate to come across just such a periodical, laying on the floor in a horrible gas station bathroom, soaking up a puddle of bodily fluids that, no doubt, contained urine, saliva, blood and liquid feces. The bathroom was so gross, Jimmy figured there were at least three other, as yet to be identified, bodily fluids congealing in that puddle and being drunk by the black and white rag called 'Abandoned Zoo Animal Shopper Emporium.' Jimmy peeled it off the floor as he dropped a deuce somewhere in the middle of Nowhere, Indiana.

There were many bears for sale. Cheap too. People buy bear cubs all the time. They set up something like Mr. Jack's Bear Zoo. They make a few bucks letting weary travelers come in to look at their sullen grizzly bear cub sitting forlorn in a tiny cage. But the bear cub gets bigger. And he wants more and more food. And he shits bigger and bigger shits. It becomes more and more dangerous to take care of him. Then, the bear becomes neglected, and the people stop coming to see the depressing bear and Jack is forced to close up shop.

Jimmy would buy Jack's full grown grizzly bear for pennies on the dollar. He'd come to Wyld Louie's where Wyld Louie would take care of that bear. That poor grizzly, who'd led a less than favorable life would not have to live that way any longer.

Wyld Louie wasn't an animal abuser. He was an animal facilitator. He'd ease the expedition of bears on their trip to bear heaven, a place much better than Jack's Bear Zoo. Of that, Jimmy was certain. Wyld Louie didn't concern himself with the ethics, he just wanted to blow up bears.

"I should bend you over and teach you a lesson, Jimmuh. Now, hold him down while I load him up." Wyld Louie set the charge on the exploding bear rig, getting into position at the bear's posterior.

"Shouldn't we tranq him first?" Jimmy asked.

"Damnit, Jimmuh. It's a friggin' black bear. This thing's more docile than my dead grandma jacked up on ludes. Just hold him so as I can get the rig up his ass."

Jimmy grasped the bear by the scruff of his neck. The bear looked at Jimmy with hopeful eyes. All he wanted was another chocolate pudding pie.

Wyld Louie took hold of the bear's stubby tail, exposing its anus, which was crusted with dried berry seeds, encased in crusted turdlettes. Wyld Louie wanted to invent bear toilet paper one day, so he didn't have to stick his hand in bear shit. It was a problem that needed solving.

The dynamite rig touched the bear's ass. The bear clenched. Jimmy felt the beast quiver. He wasn't used to that, the bears were always tranquilized. He tightened his grip. Wyld Louie applied more pressure against the anus, coaxing it open to accept the payload.

The bear grunted. Jimmy didn't like the sound of that grunt. It wasn't a small warning, it was an 'I'm about to go apeshit' warning.

Wyld Louie slammed the rig home like he was loading a shell into a Howitzer. The bear wasn't pleased about the suppository and the discomfort associated with it. The grunt became a roar. Jimmy held on like he was about to go eight seconds on a bucking bronco.

The bear thrashed its head from side to side. Jimmy held on for dear life, as he was tossed this way and that. If he let go, he'd lose the only thing keeping the bear's mouth from his body, the bear itself. As long as he held on to the bear by the back of its head, the bear couldn't chomp on his arms or the rest of him. He was a part of the bear as long as his grip held.

Wyld Louie backed up against the wall, watching Jimmy go for a ride with the raging black bear. "I think we should have tranqed it, Jimmuh!" he yelled over the din of the roaring bear.

If Jimmy lived through this, he was gonna bend Wyld Louie over and tongue lash his ass for that statement.

The bear reared up on its hindquarters. The new posturing brought Jimmy face to face with the bear. He let go of its scruff before it could bite his face off. He dropped to the floor but before he could scurry away, the bear had his right arm in its mouth.

When you think about a bear eating you, as one often does, you think it's going to be quick and painless. The bear will probably stomp you, rendering you unconscious, before he shreds you to manageable chunks of meat with his razor-sharp teeth like a great white. The opposite, Jimmy found out, was true.

The black bear didn't eat Jimmy. Instead, he gnawed on his arm like it was jerky. He bit down. The pain was incredible. Bears don't have teeth like sharks, they're closer to the teeth in a human mouth, some sharp in the front, but mostly absurdly large molars made for pulping plant matter to a macerated pulp. To the bear, Jimmy's arm probably had the consistency of a branch full of blackberries.

Jimmy cried out in pain. He looked to Wyld Louie and yelled, "Tranq it! Tranq it!"

"I can't, Jimmuh! He's got me! He's got me! Help!"

Jimmy looked down the length of the bear. Wyld Louie was caught up to his elbow in the bear's ass. Jimmy's arm wasn't the only thing it had a hold on.

Jimmy was stuck in one end of the bear and Wyld Louie was caught in the other.

Jimmy was impressed with the clamping power of the bear's muzzle, as well as its asshole. He watched Wyld Louie trying to pull his arm out of the bear's ass like he was Winnie the Pooh trying to pry a honey pot out of a tiny hole.

"Jimmuh! Jimmuh! Its asshole has got a hold of me! Help me, Jimmuh! Help me!"

"I can't help you! It's got my arm!"

"Son-of-a-bitch, Jimmuh! I'm gonna bend you over for this! I need help!"

"We gotta tranq it!"

"No time! He's gonna blow!"

The bear spun, trying to shake off both men. The rotation slammed Wyld Louie against the prep cabinets. Equipment rained down on him. He spotted the tube of lube he used on the tight assed bears. He grabbed it with his free hand and bit off the cap. He plugged the business end of the lube tube into the bear's ass and squeezed.

As the petroleum-based lube found its way into the airtight crevices between the anus and Wyld Louie's arm, his limb began to slide out like a wet turd.

The bear eased its grip, probably feeling the sensation of shitting out Wyld Louie's arm.

"Jimmuh? This thing's already loaded to blow. Bring him out into the demonstration area before he blows."

"What?"

"Damnit, Jimmuh! That bear is gonna miss the show if you don't get him out there right now. I'm not giving any refunds today. If I do, it's your ass that's gonna take a licking."

Jimmy must have been feeling delirious while being eaten by the bear because he found he was coaxing it out toward the demonstration area, letting his arm be the bait while the bear followed.

The bear suckled on his arm like it was sucking the juice of a rare sirloin through a straw. He wasn't about to let go.

Jimmy heard the roar of the crowd as he dragged the bear out into the demonstration enclosure.

'*Awww*' they all went when they saw the black bear clamped down on his arm. It was just as adorable as the ones they saw on YouTube. Jimmy saw a sea of cell phones replace the faces of the guests. They were all capturing this on video, an adorable black bear, eating a man just before it exploded.

Jimmy pushed against the side of the bear's head with his free hand. The bear's mouth didn't yield. He tried to kick the bear, but he couldn't get his leg high enough to make contact. The damned thing was going to blow any moment. Jimmy envisioned some lucky kid shellacking one of his ears to his face. He had to break free.

There was only one way out.

Jimmy got in close to the bear, almost hugging it. He looked up at the underside of the bear's mouth with his arm clamped inside it. He punched up into the bottom jaw of the bear, clamping it down harder. The additional force severed his arm from his body.

Jimmy scurried away from the bear. The bear paid Jimmy no mind. He was happy to keep his snack.

Jimmy ran out of the enclosure. He went to push the blast door shut, only to find there was no arm to push it closed with. He switched to his left (and less dominant arm) to slam the door shut.

He leaned against the door as he tried to maneuver the bolt closed with his hand before the inevitable explosion.

The bolt slammed home and he felt the giant *KA-BLAM* rattle his body through the door.

Jimmy looked at the place where his arm should be. It wasn't there. He needed to find a first aid kit.

Did Wyld Louie even have one?

Chapter 10

It was lunch time. Most of the guests were at the cafe eating while they waited for their appointed Exploding Bear Experience. Wyld Louie's Wyld Café and Toilets was part of the overall Wyld Louie's Exploding Bear Experience. The café was open for a short duration: noon until two. That meant that guests only had a two-hour window to eat, drink, piss and shit.

Yes, Wyld Louie even closed the toilets. There were two port-o-john style outhouses on the property as well. Those could be utilized anytime. Wyld Louie didn't have a regular cleaning regimen for those plastic disgust huts. They got rancid quickly and stayed that way for a long time. Usually, when Wyld Louie got sick of licking ass as punishment for bad behavior, he sent the offender to clean the outhouses.

But the toilets? They were Wyld Louie's pride and joy. Even more so than the café. Wyld Louie believed a man's shitter was a man's throne. The toilets at Wyld Louie's Wyld Café and Toilets were worthy of an emperor's bowel movements. That's why guests would hold it in until the toilets opened. The lines were longer for the bathroom than they were for the food.

And the food, well, it was forgettable fare for the most part. There were burgers (probably made with a percentage of horsemeat to keep the costs down) hot dogs (you can't add anything more nightmarish to a hot dog than there already is by default) fried chicken sandwiches (have you ever wondered what they do with the chickens they raise just to lay eggs? Visit Wyld Louie's Wyld Café and Toilets and you'll find out) and of course slices of pizza (let's not even get into that.) And, as of earlier that morning, a menu item had been added, The Borkinator Burger.

The policy was, no outside food or beverages. That, coupled with the other policy of no return entries, forced the visitors to eat at Wyld Louie's Wyld Café and Toilets or starve to death. And nobody wanted to starve to death at Wyld Louie's because he'd probably use you to feed the bears. And it wasn't out of the question that your remains might end up in the burgers.

So, if you weren't working at the café, you had a little bit of downtime during the lunch rush.

Larry had scored some weird looking mushrooms he found growing on a pile of shit behind one of the outhouses. No doubt, left there by a guest who felt mother nature was a cleaner environment to take a dump in instead of the overloaded outhouses. He thought they looked like the 'shrooms his brother used to find growing on cow shit when he was away at summer camp. His brother would harvest them and bring them home when camp ended. By then, the 'shrooms would be dried out and he and his brother would trip balls for the rest of the summer.

"You eating lunch?" Larry asked Chauncey. "I got something you may be interested in."

"What's that?" Chauncey asked, stowing away his dancing hamster in its Habitrail.

Larry held out his hand, displaying the weird looking mushrooms.

"'Shrooms?" Chauncey asked, delighted by the offering.

"Yeah. I guess. I think. Pretty sure."

"Guess we're eating 'shrooms for lunch. Didn't even know there were cows around here. Where'd you find them?"

"Right here, on property."

"Oh jeez, don't tell me Louie is blowing up cows now, trying to pass them off as bears."

"No, but I wouldn't put it past him."

Larry and Chauncey snuck off behind a small, rundown shed behind the petting zoo. It was the spot where Wyld Louie's employees often gathered to sneak a sip of booze out of an airline bottle someone had snuck in for the shift. Sometimes, they'd just go there to take a break from the tireless guests and their absurd demands. Once in a while, they'd creep back behind the shed to take a hit off someone's vape pen or take a morsel of an edible or, as in this case, pop a few 'shrooms and expand their horizons.

"You're sure these are 'shrooms, right? We're not gonna die, are we?" Chauncey asked, once again eyeing the piece of dried-up mushroom in his palm.

He'd done 'shrooms once before. Back in high school. That was like five years ago. He couldn't be certain he recalled what they looked like, especially after tripping balls on them for most of the night. He swore there was an army of French people launching gigantic cows at him because he was trying to storm their castle. In hindsight, he understood it was a hallucination he had as a result of watching Monty Python and the Holy Grail a few hours earlier.

Or was it?

He thought he remembered them being sort of brownish in color. The mushroom he had in his hand was almost green, kind of an earthy green, but what was throwing him off were the red dots. He was pretty sure he didn't remember the magic mushrooms he did before having red dots.

"Yeah man. I found them growing on shit," Larry assured him, "the magic ones always grow on shit."

Chauncey didn't know if that was true or not. He thought maybe somebody had told him that once. Larry sounded pretty sure of that fact. So fuck it. He popped it in his mouth and chewed.

Larry followed suit.

They chewed and watched one another, waiting for the other to start tripping balls. All they exchanged were sour pusses. To Chauncey, the mushroom definitely tasted like shit. Not that he had ever tasted shit before, but the flavor in his mouth could only be described as shit.

By the look on Larry's face, he was pretty sure Larry felt the same about the taste. Chauncey wanted to get high more than he wanted to spit out the crap flavored mushroom that may, or may not, be the magic variety. He forced himself to swallow and end the torture before he hurled.

Larry swallowed also.

They looked at each other.

Nothing.

Nothing.

Nothing.

Then, Chauncey watched as Larry's face began to melt off his fucking skull! Holy shit! The mushroom was melting Larry's flesh! Chauncey fucking freaked out. He grabbed the skin on his own face, pushing it desperately against his skull, trying to keep it from melting off. He was pretty sure he was screaming, but he sounded like a robot chicken.

Larry melted into a blob that still looked like Larry. Then Larry screamed like a robot chicken and tackled Chauncey to the ground. Chauncey cried like a robot chicken, saying things like, "Don't eat me Blob Larry! *BOK*!" And, "I am not your chicken feed, bitch! *BOK*!" Also, "Larry, you chicken-fried-chicken-ass-blob, I'm gonna eat you like I ordered you at 2am, drunk at IHOP on a Tuesday! *BOK*!"

Blob Larry was all like, "Dude, mellow your high, bro. I'm not eating you. Fucking look at the colors man. The fucking colors are mother earth and we are her babies and we shit upon her earth and we need diapers and mother earth has had it up to here with our shit and mother earth needs a glass of wine and bro, I'm tripping balls so bad i can't capitalize anything im saying right now and i cant punctuate anything im saying and my autlcerrect stoped werking. fuck thi is md trppyi."

Chauncey got a grip on his high. He wanted to be tripping balls the way Larry was. He was at peace with his grammatic abnormalities. He wanted to experience that kind of high, where the rules didn't matter, and everything wrong felt right. The colors began to wash over him. First the pinks, calming pinks. Then the blue, centering blues. Now greens washed past, baking the earth in mellow. Larry congealed into a purple person, no longer a blob. He was beautiful.

"Larry," Chauncey said, relaxed, "you're beautiful, man. Beautiful and purple."

"Chauncey, you sound like a robot chicken, my dude. And that is marvelous. We should all be robot chicken people. That would be glorious."

Larry began scratching his foot on the ground, looking for bugs. Chauncey became the robot chicken he sounded like, also. He found a bug and pecked at it with his mouth. He ate a grub. It tasted like a gummy bear. Purple, chocolate gummy bears provided by mother nature mother nature who didn't capitalize anything or use   punctuation andstoppedusingthefuckingspacebarbecausethespacebar hasalotofstressinitslifeanditneedsabreakeverynowndthn vwls nd brk vry nw nd thn ls

No rules were amazing. Chauncey wanted to make more rules go away.

"Dude, let's go to the café and walk in not wearing a shirt or shoes and get service anyway. Fucking rules make mother nature so sad."

Purple Larry loved that idea. "Yeah. And let's, like, eat a whole bunch of stuff and then go swimming right away. That is the worst rule, bro!"

"Oh gawd yea! And let's put e before i even after c. Who says words can't still be words? Why does e always need to take a backseat unless c is around? And why is c so intolerant?"

"That's what I'm talking about, bro! You know what we should do? We should totally rewrite the ten commandments, so they are way more cooler. It would be like we can start our own new religions and it would be the cool religion and people would wanna do our religion all the time and we could be priests. And we could be popes. And we could be gods."

"I've always wanted to be gods," Chauncey said.

"Yeah, me too."

"Let's be gods."

"Let's do it!"

Larry and Chauncey came out of their hiding spot behind the petting zoo.

Larry tapped Chauncey on the shoulder and pointed to the front door of the equipment shed. "That's where they hide the god-making stuff."

"And shovels," Chauncey said.

"Gods are made of shovels."

"You're right."

They went to the shed to get the god-making shovels. There were two shovels in the shed. Well, there was one shovel and one long-handled scoop. Both were used to pick up shit. But what Larry and Chauncey saw were god-making shovels of gold. They gleamed like they came from mother nature. Mother nature, who never used capital letters and never used punctuation andstoppedusingthespacebartogiveitabreakeverynowand then

"How do they work?" Chauncey asked Larry, holding one of the golden god-making shovels.

"We need to melt them into god-armor."

Larry and Chauncey melted their god-making shovels into god-armor. They adorned themselves in the blessed pieces of armor. They were now gods.

"You look like a god, bro," Purple Larry god said.

"You look like a god, too. A purple god," Chauncey god said.

"We can fly now."

"Yes, we can."

"Let's fly!"

Larry and Chauncey soared through the heavens. Anyone not tripping balls like they were would have seen them rolling around on the ground, getting dirty.

"Let's stop flying and get some steeds," Larry said.

"We totally need steeds. Gods have steeds."

"There's some steeds over there," Larry said, pointing to the dancing hamster Habitrail cage.

"Oh man. That's my dancing hamster," Chauncey said. "He dances, you know?"

"Does he steed?"

"He steeds indeed."

"Let's go steed him."

Larry and Chauncey went to retrieve the dancing steed from the Habitrail.

Lunch time was coming to a close at the café. The guests who had crapped and eaten (in that order) began to wander back out onto the grounds of Wyld Louie's Exploding Bear Experience. A few of them made their way to the petting zoo.

A man and his son, a kid named Wilson, were the first to return to the petting zoo. They stopped to ask the two guys, who were tripping balls and riding a dancing hamster, if they'd seen a guy named Harry with a beaver.

The guy who rode on the front of the dancing hamster pulled a shovel, which was stuffed down the back of his pants, its spade crusted in shit, and held it aloft like a sword. "Alas, I've not seen the mortal named Harry, nor his trusty beaver steed."

The father winced. He thought the two of them might have been tripping balls. "Well, what about a big man? His name is Angel."

Chauncey, who was riding on the back of the dancing hamster, which was, as near as the man could tell, squished to death under the weight of the two stoners, panicked at the mention of Angel's name. "Angel? There are angels around here? Gods hate angels. We've gotta get outta here Purple Larry god!"

Larry picked up the dead dancing hamster and threw it across the expanse of the petting zoo. It soared through the air and slapped against the side of the shed.

"Wee!" the two of them said, as if they were riding on the back of the dead hamster Larry had just thrown.

"C'mon, Wilson. We've gotta find Angel," his dad said, taking his son by the hand.

The two guys screamed like little girls and ran away.

Chapter 11

After Wyld Louie's Wyld Café and Toilets closed for the day, Wyld Louie had a bit more free time in the remainder of the day. That's when Jenny planned to strike. Between the 2 o'clock closing of the café and the 3 o'clock exploding bear demonstration, Wyld Louie took his lunch break.

Most days, Wyld Louie tucked himself away in his office, next to Jenny's office. What he did there was anybody's guess. Well, not really. One thing everybody knew he did in there was lick the asses of out-of-control employees to get them back in line. Jenny knew what went on in there, but she had never experienced the thrill.

Jenny longed for a thorough tongue bath from Wyld Louie. She wanted to be a bad employee. So bad. The baddest girl. She wanted to be spanked and licked and spanked again, then licked more and called Jennuh while she was learning her lesson. Lesson after lesson. She wanted multiple lessons. She would learn her lesson for sure. She wanted Wyld Louie to see her lesson-learning face.

Jimmy, who didn't have to work the lunch shift at the café, did as she instructed. He cleared off Wyld Louie's Wyld Desk, placed a fancy linen tablecloth on top of it, adorned it with two place settings, candles, and a lotus flower floating in a crystal glass half-filled with purified water. He set Wyld Louie's Wyld Bluetooth speaker (available for purchase in Wyld Louie's Wyld Gift Shop) in the corner, softly playing music that was both romantic and wild. Barry Manilow, obviously.

Jenny paced, waiting for Wyld Louie to lock up the toilets for the day and return to his office. She heard him coming down the hallway. She caught her breath. This was really going to happen. She wanted to pee, eager with excited anticipation.

"Jennuh!" Wyld Louie said, being short with her. No doubt, tired from the morning rush and looking forward to his personal time for the next hour.

"Hi, Wyld Louie. I hope you're hungry. I made something special for you for lunch today."

"Ugh, Jennuh. Not today. I'm tired. I just want to sit in my office for a spell. Have a bite of my sangwich (he actually says sangwich, not sandwich) and maybe watch something a little spicy on my phone. Hold all my calls, Jennuh."

Jenny's heart sank. Her fish was about to jump off the hook.

"Wait! Just, please, I've done something special for you. I promise it'll be relaxing. I'll do all the work, I swear. You'll be relaxed when it's all over."

Wyld Louie stopped in his tracks before his hand hit the knob to his office door. "What in the hell are you talking about, Jennuh?"

"I wanna be bad for you."

This was it. He was gonna get angry with her and insist on correcting her behavior the Wyld Louie way.

"Jennuh, you on drugs?"

"I dunno, would it upset you if I were on drugs?"

"Damnit, Jennuh! Yeah, it would upset me if you were on drugs. You know what I'd have to do to you if you were on drugs?"

Jenny's eyes widened like she was a female lead in a manga book. "You'd lick my ass, wouldn't you?"

Wyld Louie's face turned to disgust. "What? No, I'd be forced to let you go. I can't have druggies working for me. That's very unchristian like."

Jenny was exasperated. Unchristian like? Since when did Wyld Louie follow the way of the Lord? He spent his days exploding God's creatures for the gratification of sinners. And, getting fired for taking drugs? Didn't Wyld Louie know that Jenny was probably the *only* one working for him that wasn't taking drugs?

She prayed to God. What? Dear sweet baby Jesus in Heaven above, what, pray-tell, could she do to get this man upset enough to lick her ass?

"Why won't you get mad at me?!" Jenny demanded.

Wyld Louie froze. Jenny had never yelled at him before. Nobody had ever yelled at him before. Wyld Louie did the yelling around here. He didn't know what to say. How could he? He couldn't tell her that the reason he could never yell at her, get mad at or raise his voice to her was that he thought she was the most beautiful girl in the world. He was incapable of being angry at someone so pretty. He was helpless to do anything but let her do whatever she wanted because he had warm feelings for her.

He'd tried to put up a facade of bravado. He'd pretend to be cross with her, lower his voice an octave and say things like, "Damnit, Jennuh." But he'd never dare take her to his office for a behavior correcting ass licking. That would be unchristian like.

"Jennuh, can't I just eat my lunch in peace?"

Jenny started to cry and said, "Go on. It doesn't matter anyway. I don't care."

Wyld Louie hated to see her cry. Was he the reason she was crying? He tried so hard to not be a jerk to her. He felt awful. He didn't know what to say. He put his head down and walked into his office.

The sultry, seductive and savage sounds of Barry Manilow washed over him as he walked into his office. He loved Barry Manilow.

"I love Barruh Maniluh," he said aloud.

His jaw dropped when he saw his desk. What the fuck was going on? Was this a prank?

"Jennuh, who was in my fucking office?! I'm gonna lick their fucking ass raw!"

He turned.

Jenny was right behind him. She looked into his eyes with desperation and said, "I was in your office."

Wyld Louie looked back into her eyes. He understood something he didn't understand before. Jenny needed to be punished.

Chapter 12

Barney was put to the task of securing a new bear for the next demonstration.

Wyld Louie picked him since he was the idiot who brought the dingo dog to the petting zoo. If Barney could manage a rabid canine, he could deal with a dang bear.

Barney had no idea where Jimmy even kept the bears, let alone how to wrangle the damn things. He was poking around the petting zoo, looking in the shed when he saw a bunched-up plastic baggie. Out of curiosity, he picked it up and found a few pieces of dried-up mushrooms inside.

Barney hadn't done 'shrooms in a while. He popped one in his mouth and tucked it up between his lip and gums. He figured maybe the magic mushroom would open a world of possibilities in his hunt for the exploding bears.

Jimmy had not been keeping the exploding bears in the shed. Barney moved his search outward. The colors began to wash over him. The 'shroom was kicking in. It was euphoric.

Wyld Louie's became an ocean of possibilities, liminal spaces and other places. Barney knew how to take the trip. He centered his Chi and went along for the ride. The 'shroom blew his mind like no other 'shroom before it.

He soared over Wyld Louie's Exploding Bear Experience like a drone. The wind whooshed against his face and forced his eyes open wider. His eyes grew bear seeking radar dishes. They scanned the world for the exploding bears. He saw bugs and he saw asparagus, he saw orangutans eating banana bread and having tea klatches. He did not see any bears.

He flew on, beyond the confines of Wyld Louie's and on to other lands. Other worlds. He soared over the jungles of Themopolis where he waved at a family of friendly orange friars and yellow monks with bad toupees. No bears.

His drone body aimed star ward. In space he battled wiggly, wobbly space worms who shot at him with plasma balls, and he shot back with love. The love nailed one of the space worms in the eye and he turned into cupid and shot heart-tipped arrows into his other space worm friends who all turned into rainbows and sailed across the galaxy. No bears.

His weightless body splashed down into the ocean. His bear-seeking radar eyes spotted a pod of wild exploding bears. He homed in on them like a torpedo and plucked one out of the water. It was wet. Barney would have to dry it off so it could explode. He'd do that as soon as he stopped tripping balls.

Barney flew with his wet exploding bear back to Wyld Louie's.

Once he returned to Wyld Louie's, psychologically speaking, he realized he had some work to do to get this bear ready for the show. He sighed.

A half hour later, Wyld Louie was yelling at Barney. "Jeezus, King of Rice! What in the hell is that thing, Barnuh?"

"An exploding bear," Barney said, "and it's Barney, sir. Not Barhuh."

"Damnit, Barnuh! I said Barnuh! What don't you understand about Barnuh? You're lucky my tongue feels like it ran the Indianapolis 500, or I'd have you bend over and I'd lick your ass three ways to Wednesduh!"

The door to Wyld Louie's office opened. Jenny popped her head out. She winked at Wyld Louie and closed the door really quick.

Wyld Louie blushed and changed the subject back to the bear. "What kind of bear did you say this is, Barnuh?"

Barney looked at the bear. He wasn't sure. He had done his best to make the bear look more like a bear. He found some sticks and strapped them around the bear's body to give it legs like a bear, since the bear he found didn't really have legs. Then he took a paper plate from the café, cut it in half, and nailed each semicircle to the bear's head since his bear didn't have bear ears in the traditional sense of bear ears. He didn't really see any ears at all on the creature.

Barney was actually a little bit concerned that he'd picked up a unicorn snake mermaid and not a bear. "It's a, umm, water bear, sir."

"Damnit, Barnuh! This is a fucking narwhal with a paper plate nailed to the top of its head! And what's with the sticks?"

"That's his legs, sir."

"Damnit, Barnuh! I can't blow this thing up! Do narwhal's even have asses?"

"It's a water bear, sir. And water bears have asses. All bears do."

The narwhal flopped around, trying to wiggle back to the ocean and away from the psychotic people trying to blow it up.

"He's as ornery as a bear, I'll give him that. Okay, Barnuh, hand me that tranq gun so I can settle him down and get him loaded for the next show."

Wyld Louie fired 500 cc's of Ketamine into the creature. It fell asleep in no time at all.

Wyld Louie grabbed the exploding bear rig and went about looking for its butt hole.

"Damnit, Barnuh! I can't find a butt hole anywhere on this thing! You sure it has a butt hole?"

Barney looked around. "Oh, here it is!" he said, pointing at the blowhole on top of the narwhal's head.

Wyld Louie said, "Hell of a place for a butt hole. This is a water bear, you say?"

"Yeah," Barney said.

"Well, okay. Get your water bear out there for the show, he's ready to go."

Wyld Louie returned to his office and closed the door behind him.

Barney scratched his head. He wasn't sure how he was going to get the water bear out into the demonstration enclosure. He wasn't even sure he knew how he got the fucking thing here in the first place.

Chapter 13

Jimmy needed to get back in the game. Barney was fucking up big time. Wyld Louie was growing impatient. At least three of the guests figured out the last bear that exploded wasn't really a bear.

They had no idea what it was. Jimmy wasn't sure himself. Barney kept telling everyone it was a water bear. Jimmy would have to Google it to find out if it was real, but he couldn't afford one of those fancy smart phones.

Didn't matter if water bears were real or not. Whatever that thing was, it was fucking nasty when it exploded. It was the fattiest bear they'd blown up yet. There wasn't much in the way of meat to salvage for the Borkinator burgers. It was all lard.

What made matters worse was that only one guest bought adhesive after the demonstration. Most guests were covered in slimy, foul smelling, charred lard. Jimmy smelled what could only be described as burnt sardine bacon. No wonder nobody, save for one customer, wanted to shellac that stuff to their body. The one lucky guest who got a decent bear part in him, got the weirdest part of the water bear, its unicorn horn, impaled in his crotch. He was proud, swinging that long hard thing around at the other guests for the rest of the day. Shellacked forever (or 8 to 12 weeks) to his crotch, a far better member than the one that dangled there before it.

"You need to get back in the game, Jimmuh. I can't be losing sales like this. Barnuh is bringing in the worst bears for blowing up. If it keeps up like this, I won't be able to pay anybody, except myself, of course."

"I've got no arm, Wyld Louie."

"Dammit, Jimmuh. Arms grow back. Put it in a bucket of cow manure or something and get it growing faster."

"I don't think it works that way. I don't think my arm is going to grow back at all."

"Dammit, Jimmuh, people grow back arms all the time. I saw it in the National Geographic, or something. I need you, Jimmuh. I need you badly.

Go get that arm growing. I'm going to be in my office."

Wyld Louie walked back to his office and slammed the door shut.

Jimmy wondered how things went with Jenny's plan. He hadn't seen her since he set everything up for her in Wyld Louie's office. If anyone was smart enough to know how to grow an arm back fast, it would be Jenny.

Maybe she was out in the woods looking for a better bear too. She was proactive that way. A real company woman.

Jimmy wandered into the woods. He hoped he would run into a black bear. He knew they were docile, but after getting mauled and maimed by the last one, he felt skittish on the hunt. That must be what a one-armed diver on Shark Week feels like after a hammerhead bites off an arm. One second you could be making sweet, sweet love to the fish, and the next thing you know, instinct kicks in and you're down a limb. Mother nature was strange like that. They say love is love, but try telling that to sharks and bears.

The woods are a lonely place. Jimmy was a lonely man walking around a lonely place, living a lonely life. He longed for companionship. At times like these, stuck in his head, looking through the forest for Jenny, a bear, or even a stray arm, he felt it worse. Wyld Louie's was a distraction from the fact that his life had not gone the way he'd dreamed it would as a little boy.

Wyld Louie's provided Jimmy with a purpose. Most of the other guys working here were directionless burnouts. Wyld Louie's was their only option. Jimmy didn't drink or trip balls. He wanted to do better for himself, but he didn't know how. At Wyld Louie's he was useful, he was somebody. Without bears, Wyld Louie's was just a hapless roadside petting zoo with bad food and absurd gifts.

Jimmy was the guy that brought the magic to the park. He was Wyld Louie's lifeblood. At least as much as Wyld Louie and Jenny were. So now, down an arm, he might as well give up, drop acid, drink swill and not give a fuck.

But that wasn't him. Jimmy wasn't a quitter.

He didn't need Jenny to hold his hand like a mom. He could figure this arm thing out. He was going to get this done and get back on that horse. He was going to dive into the ocean and bang that hammerhead shark again. He was going to find an arm and fuck up a black bear!

Jimmy stormed back to Wyld Louie's. He knew where he was going to find his arm. He stormed the observation platform, quiet now that they were between shows. He walked up to the railing and hopped into the pit around the enclosure that kept hostile bears from accessing the platform loaded with paying customers.

The pit, Jimmy knew, was strewn with bear parts that didn't get blasted onto the observation platform. There were bear ears, bear toes, bear snouts and, of course, bear arms. He rummaged through the available dismembered arms looking for just the right one.

He knew it when he saw it: his new arm. A black bear's arm. Blown off from the exact spot his arm had been chewed off. A perfect fit!

Jimmy grabbed the bear arm like it was a brand-new toy he'd been waiting for at the toy store, and he rushed to the bear preparation area the way that a boy would rush the new toy to the cashier's checkout counter.

It wasn't easy to do with only one intact arm, but Jimmy positioned the arm against his stub and used the staple gun Wyld Louie used to tack the daily exploding bear schedule to his cork board.

Snap! Snap! Snap! Snap! Snap!

Five staples held the bear arm where his old arm used to be.

He shored it up with a roll of duct tape. That sucker wasn't going anywhere.

Now, he had a new arm. He just couldn't use it. Not yet. Jimmy wasn't a quitter. He was going to get his new bear arm working as good as his old arm. He had to think like a bear. Be the bear.

Be the bear!

Jimmy flexed his new arm with his mind like he was trying out some new Jedi mind trick. His bear arm hung, lifeless as an old man's dick. He wasn't a quitter, he tried again. He grimaced, trying harder. He clenched his sphincter tight, almost causing it to implode on itself. Still, his new arm dangled like an old Christmas tree ornament.

Beads of sweat formed along his brow. He flexed once more. The arm twitched but only because he wiggled his shoulder a little bit. No, that was cheating, the arm didn't really move.

"Fuck," Jimmy said.

Maybe the arm had been laying in the pit too long. It did have a certain tang to it that Jimmy figured was natural bear funk, but it could be the scent of rigor mortis setting in. He reached for the staple remover, defeated.

He was about to consider himself a quitter when Barney entered with a new bear in tow.

Jimmy was impressed. The dope looked like he had wrangled a genuine bear. The bear was less than impressed with Jimmy. It growled at him the moment it laid eyes on him.

Jimmy's heart leapt into his throat. The fear he felt when the other bear mauled him was the same fear he felt now. Was this the son of the black bear that took his arm and blew up, come to have its revenge because he was made an orphan?

Jimmy heard a declaration of the bear's quest come to its end in his growl. "My name is Beardigo Montoya. You blew up my father. Prepare to die," it *Grrrrr*ed.

"Holy Fuck! Tranq it! Tranq it!" Jimmy yelled at Barney.

Barney, who'd just figured out how to wrangle a bear, hadn't figured out how to subdue a bear once you figured out step one. "What's a tranq?" he asked.

"The gun! The gun!" Jimmy yelled.

The bear snorted and scratched an angry paw along the floor like a bull ready to charge.

Barney grabbed the gun and tossed it to Jimmy. Jimmy caught it with his good hand, looked at it and said, "You asshole, not a staple gun! A tranquilizer gun!"

"Which one is that?!" Barney asked.

Jimmy nodded to the rifle on the wall and said, "That one! That one!"

Barney laughed. "Oh, the Special K gun?"

Jimmy backed up another step, making room between him and the revenge bear, but closing the gap between him and the wall. There was no escape. "Special K? What the fuck? No, the gun right there on the wall."

Barney laughed again. "Yeah, that's the Special K gun. Why do you want that one? There's nothing left in it. Me and Larry shot up the last of the needles last night."

"You're shooting up Ketamine?" Jimmy cried, his hope for tranquilizing the bear now lost.

Barney giggled. "It really fucks you up, man."

"No shit, asshole! Its fucking bear tranquilizer!"

"Nice," Barney said.

The bear charged Jimmy. Jimmy had nowhere to go. He placed one foot in front of the other and took a boxer's stance, his good arm holding back the only jab he had.

The bear reared up on its hindquarters and took an angry swipe at Jimmy. Jimmy ducked, bounced back up and jabbed the bear with his good arm. The punch landed but did no damage.

The bear started to sniff furiously. Its snout followed the scent to Jimmy's new arm. Once it took in a full whiff of the bear arm secured to his stump, it roared and readied another swipe with its massive front paw.

Jimmy spazzed, swinging his stump at the bear. The motion brought the limp bear arm around like a whip and it smacked the bear across the snout. The dead claws on the arm tore open a gash across the bear's nose.

The black bear yelped and retreated, dropping to all fours and moaning like a cracked-out hooker getting her fix.

Holy shit! Jimmy realized the best way to battle a bear is to become a bear yourself. His alpha bear arm had fucked up the raging bear. It slinked out of the room and ran wildly out into Wyld Louie's Exploding Bear Experience.

Jimmy had solved one problem, but now he had another one on his hands, which he now had two of again.

"C'mon!" Jimmy said to Barney.

"Where are we going?"

"We've got a wild, rampaging bear to take out." Jimmy shrugged his shoulder and his new bear arm flopped around in a 'follow me' wave as he ran out the door.

Chapter 14

"Hello? Yes, I need a beaver," Harry said and paused as he listened to the voice on the other end of the line process his request. "No, it has to be alive, or a giant Angel is going to kill me."

Harry listened again. "No! I didn't take Larry's magic mushrooms again!"

Pause.

"A big, black Angel. That's what I said."

Pause.

"No, I'm not racist. He's a black guy, named Angel."

Pause.

"I have no idea what the color of his skin has to do with anything, I was just trying to paint a picture for you."

Pause.

"No! I'm not really painting you a picture. It was a figure of speech."

Pause.

"Wow, why are you getting so hung up on this black thing? Maybe you're the one who's racist?"

Pause.

"Oh, sorry. Latino, not racist. I get confused sometimes."

Pause.

"No! I don't think that just because you're Latino that you can't catch a beaver. Where did you even get that from?"

Pause.

"What? No! Where did that even come from? I'm not transphobic! I'll bang a dude right now and prove it, if I have to!"

Pause.

"Look, I have no idea who trans people sleep with, I was just saying..."

Pause.

"Wait? Closeted feelings? No, it's just, sometimes, when I'm alone at night I think about... things. Hmm, maybe I am gay."

Harry shook his head. "What does any of this have to do with beavers, anyway? Can you get me one or not?"

Pause.

"Oh, sorry, Dad. I must've dialed the wrong number."

Harry hung up the phone. Break time was almost over. That guy, Angel, would be back soon and he still didn't have a beaver. Where the fuck was he supposed to get a beaver on such short notice?

Plus, what was the big deal anyway? He'd been using the shaved porcupine for months after the actual beaver kicked the bucket. Turns out beavers can catch dry ass, a rare condition brought on by incessant licking of their assholes. The gasket around their anus dries up and they can no longer pucker it shut and all the shit comes out and then all their intestines come out since they can't stop the flow. Eventually, they shit out their entire insides and die. Only beavers suffer from it since their asses naturally taste good. Sometimes God works in mysterious and cruel ways.

Harry was happy his ass didn't taste good.

It was a happy accident that the porcupine's ass tasted decent. Harry had no idea what a porcupine's ass tasted like, and he wasn't about to find out, either. He figured a porcupine was roughly the size of a beaver, and if he mowed their stabby quills, nobody would notice. As far as the strawberry ass flavor, he was going to depend on the power of suggestion to overcome that hurdle.

It worked, too. Right up until that meddling kid and his dad showed up with that massive Angel guy in tow.

Harry wandered into the woods. The patch of forest that Wyld Louie's Exploding Bear Experience was nestled among was loaded with woodland creatures. There weren't any streams around so he probably wouldn't be lucky enough to come across a beaver, but there had to be some sort of critter that he could pass off as a beaver.

Porcupines were out of the question, but maybe he could paint a raccoon or a squirrel and make it passable. If there was one thing in life Harry had learned, it's that there's always a path around obstacles. No beaver? Shave a porcupine. Can't use a porcupine? It doesn't matter if you only have an elephant. Roll him around in the mud and tell everyone it's a saber-toothed beaver. And believe it when you say it.

Harry heard rustling beyond a deadfall. He crept up to the downed tree, careful not to step on a twig or crunch a dead leaf underfoot. This could be it, his new beaver.

Like a mountain lion, he silently prowled along the deadfall and found his prey. A beaver! Sorta.

Harry was impressed. It was fat, furry, and brown. The critter was only missing giant bucked teeth and a flat frying pan tail. Other than that, this was his beaver. Harry pounced and caught the would-be beaver. The tiny monster struggled at first but soon tired and capitulated to its capture.

Harry had his new beaver set up at his station at the petting zoo just before the café closed for the day and the guests returned. Of course, the big bad Angel and his posse were the first to arrive.

"We're ready for our refund." Angel crossed his massive guns across his mountainside chest.

"Yes, everything is in order. Step right up and enjoy a complimentary lick of this here, genuine, beaver's ass. Strawberry flavored heaven awaits!" Harry cast both arms toward his new beaver like he was welcoming the dissatisfied customers aboard a yacht.

Angel looked at the new beaver, then looked at Wilson's dad and said, "What do you think?"

"It's a lot fuzzier," the dad said.

"He's really cute, Dad! Can I go lick his ass?" asked Wilson

His dad looked at Angel. Angel gave him a nod. "Go ahead, Wilson."

Wilson ran up to the new beaver, closed his eyes, stuck out his tongue, and licked around the anus like Winnie the Pooh licking honey from around the hole of a beehive.

Wilson's eyes lit up. "Whoa! That *really does* taste like strawberries!"

Harry wiped a bead of sweat off his brow.

Chapter 15

Harry looked impressed. Jimmy tried to flex his new bear arm, but found the muscles were still atrophied. He was going to need to loosen his new appendage. He needed physical therapy.

This required a movie montage!

A bell tolled.

Harry smiled. "I'll go wrangle up a bear for the next show while you get that arm up to snuff."

Harry set off in search of a bear for the next show. The bell tolled again. Jimmy smiled. Trumpets sounded. They were awe-inspiring.

Larry ran at the fourth wall (it was different than the other three walls) and shoved his face up close to it and said, "It's time," he paused, dramatically, "to bear arms."

Music started playing. It was filled with brassy synthesizers and wailing electric guitar riffs. A bass line got Jimmy's feet marching. He dropped to his chest and began doing one-armed, bear-armed, push-ups in time with the punishing drumbeat.

A bead of sweat formed on his brow as he worked his new arm. The sweat rolled down the ridge of his brow and dropped off his face onto the floor.

Jimmy suddenly found himself in the petting zoo. He was curling Harry's false beaver like it was a dumbbell. Harry high-fived Jimmy's good hand. A small crowd gathered around them in a semi-circle, jumping and cheering Jimmy on. The 80s synth wave guitar rager played on.

In the blink of an eye, Jimmy was using his mighty bear arm to one hand press Harry over his head. Two girls, wearing neon string bikinis (one hot pink, the other blinding yellow) pressed into Jimmy, jiggling their surgically enhanced breasts for the gratuitous pleasure of everyone who watched, while they ogled Jimmy with suggestive smiles. Jenny raced up to Jimmy, from seemingly nowhere, and offered him a sip of water from a plastic sports bottle as he pushed Harry skyward once more.

The bikini girls were gone, and Jimmy was running through the forest. He was wearing a headband, grey sweatpants, and a white t-shirt with the arms cut off. The shirt accentuated his jacked-up bear arm. As he ran, his arms pumped in time to the ripping montage music that still played from everywhere and nowhere.

Jimmy rounded a tree and hurdled a fallen log before coming face to face with an out-of-place grizzly bear. The grizzly reared up on its hind legs and roared, daring Jimmy to cross his path.

The music stopped.

Jimmy snickered. He reared back with his bear arm and walloped the inexplicable grizzly bear in the snout.

The music kicked back in as the grizzly whimpered and scurried away into the woods.

Jimmy raced toward a large boulder that jutted out from the edge of a lake in the middle of the forest. The tempo of the searing music quickened in time.

Jimmy dashed forward and leaped through the air, landing atop the large boulder. He raised his bear arm into the air. The music went ape shit berserk as Jimmy screamed like a victorious warrior. A bolt of lightning shot down out of the cloudless sky and met his bear fist.

The day exploded into white light. The music ceased in the explosion.

Jimmy found himself backstage at Wyld Louie's, face to face with a fat, hairy man wearing assless leather chaps, leather suspenders, and black leather motorcycle boots.

"Who the fuck are you?" Jimmy asked.

Harry stepped out from behind the enormous leather-clad man and said, "He's the bear."

Chapter 16

Jimmy combed his bear hand through his hair. "That's a man, not a bear!"

"I am too a bear," the half-naked man on a leash said.

Jimmy sighed and said, "Harry, did you give this guy any of those mushrooms?"

"Nah, man. The dude is as hairy as a bear. He insists he's a bear. Must be a bear. No?"

"No!" Jimmy almost swatted Harry with his bear arm before he stopped himself. He'd maul Harry if he connected with his ursine arm.

"I'm part of a whole community of bears and cubs," the hairy, half-naked man said.

"Harry, we can't blow up people. It's unethical." Larry crossed his bear arm and regular arm across his chest like a stern father.

Wyld Louie sauntered in whistling *Dixie*. "Damnit, Jimmuh! Where'd you find that mangey polar bear?"

"It's not a bear, Wyld Louie, sir," Jimmy said.

Harry shrugged. "He says he's a bear."

Wyld Louie scratched the stubble on his chin. "The bear told you it was a bear, Harruh?"

"His name is Harry, not Harruh, silly goose," the half-naked man said.

"Damnit, bear! I said Harruh! What's the matter with you, that mange get in your ears, you bald ass polar bear? I should lick your diseased ass right here before I blow you the hell up!"

"Oh! Don't threaten me with a good time," the half-naked man said, testing the limits of the leash.

Wyld Louie backed up a step. "Damnit, Jimmuh. Haven't you tranquilized that thing yet?"

"Wyld Louie, sir. I swear. This isn't a bear. It's a man. A half-naked, hairy, man. We can't blow him up."

Wyld Louie dismissed Jimmy's assertion with a wave of his hand. "Damnit, Jimmuh! The bear says it's a bear. A bear ought to know if a bear is a bear. It's a dang bear, Jimmuh. Plain as day. I can see it with my own two eyes."

Jimmy opened his mouth to protest again, but Wyld Louie held up his hand, imploring Jimmy to save his breath.

"Harruh," Wyld Louie said, "get him loaded up for the next show. Time's a wastin'."

Jimmy couldn't believe what he was witnessing. The bear was clearly a man, even if the man insisted he was a bear. A poem from Jimmy's childhood came to mind. "Fuzzy Wuzzy was a bear. Fuzzy Wuzzy had no hair," Jimmy said, reciting it out loud.

Wyld Louie picked up the tranquilizer gun and shot a dart into the bear's bare ass. The bear flinched when the dart hit home. The half-naked bear man looked over his shoulder and winked at Wyld Louie.

"Ohh, you do know how to party," The half-naked bear guy cooed.

"Fuzzy Wuzzy wasn't very fuzzy, was he?" Jimmy continued.

Wyld Louie ignored Jimmy. "Okay, Harruh, he's off to la-la land. Set the load in him."

Harry grabbed the explosive device and a rubber glove. He shoved his hand inside the rubber glove with a *snap*. He gave two pumps on a bottle of lubricant and smeared it good around the bear bomb and his gloved hand.

"'Atta boy, Harruh. Jimmuh has trained you really good. Now, slide it on into his anus, there."

Harry nodded, pulling aside one of the man's ass cheeks. He lubed up the entry with his gloved finger and lined up the explosive device for entry.

The half-naked man moaned. He was either in a drug-induced daze or sex-crazed ecstasy. Jimmy's eye went wide when he saw the half-naked man push into the device instead of Harry pushing the device into him.

Jimmy recalled further verses of the Fuzzy Wuzzy poem. "Silly Willy was a worm. Silly Willy wouldn't squirm."

There was a wet *plop* and an erotic gasp as the bomb settled inside the half-naked man.

"...Silly Willy wasn't silly. No, by gosh, he wasn't really," Jimmy said.

"Nice work, Harruh," Wyld Louie said, slapping Harry on the back.

"Mmm, very nice work," the half-naked man purred, "you can load me anytime you want, Harruh."

Wyld Louie steamed. "Damnit, bear! I said Harruh, not Harruh! I'd lick your ass ten ways to Tuesday if you weren't already ready to blow! Get on out there! It's showtime."

"I'm ready to blow alright," the half-naked man whispered in his bedroom voice as Harry led him by his leash to the demonstration area.

Chapter 17

Jenny heard the noise first. It wasn't the sound of an exploding bear. That sound was a deep, dull, *thud.* This sound was sustained and had a cadence to it. It was coming from outside Wyld Louie's Exploding Bear Experience, not inside.

Jenny got up from her desk. Her head swooned. She was still love drunk from her lunch date with Wyld Louie. He was ravenous. Insatiable. He mauled her like a bear. His passion was ursine. Wyld Louie was an animal.

She knew he would be. All those ass lickings he handed out day after day, hour after hour. All under the guise of punishment for less than favorable employee behavior. And not one of his bumbling band of nitwits ever corrected that behavior. Do you know why? Jenny knew why: Because a thorough tongue lashing from Wyld Louie was nothing less than pure ecstasy. It was the only possible explanation.

Jenny had tried to be a fuck up. Nothing worked. She couldn't get her ass reamed for the life of her. But she changed tactics and went for Wyld Louie's softer side and found an opening. And boy howdy, did Jenny open him up.

They made love front ways, back ways, sideways and in six different dimensions inside his office. It was a miraculous lunch break.

But, for all the different positions and varied pieces of office furniture they utilized, Wyld Louie still didn't lick her ass. For all her fulfillment, Jenny was left wanting where she desired it most.

Jenny peeked through the blinds of the office window that looked out upon the front entrance to Wyld Louie's. She gasped. A large crowd had gathered. Various signs poked up from the throng with messages and symbols and red circles with crosses through the middle.

It was a protest.

Jenny was aghast. Wyld Louie's had never been protested before. Everyone loved to come see the bears explode. Ethics were laid aside when it came to watching a bear get blown to bits. It was like paying to watch a massive twenty car pile-up. Everyone thinks it's horrible, but everyone wants to be first in line to pay for a front row seat to watch the carnage.

So what the hell was this protest about?

Jenny scanned some of the messages on the signs.

BEARS ARE PEOPLE TOO, one read.

BEARS ARE NOT ANIMALS, read another.

I EAT BEARS, read another. The crowd around the person holding that sign was especially thick.

Wyld Louie must have heard the ruckus too. Jenny jumped when he asked, "What the hell is going on out there, Jennuh?"

"There's a protest," Jenny said.

"A protest?" Wyld Louie asked. "What the hell are they protesting out in front of my place for? They're going to scare away all the paying customers."

"I think that's the point, baby," Jenny said, risking a pet name while they were alone.

"Babuh? Don't babuh me, babuh. Sweet talking isn't going to get me to calm down about a protest out in front of my place. Damnit, I've got to find Jimmuh and get him to chase those protesters away."

Wyld Louie stomped out of the office. Jenny sighed. She still didn't feel like she'd won Wyld Louie over after the magical afternoon they shared.

She cursed. She should've told Wyld Louie she said baby, not babuh. That would've gotten her an ass licking for sure. She loved the big oaf too much to correct him over his adorable speech impediment. It wouldn't have been a Jenny-like thing to do.

Jennuh she corrected herself in her own mind. She smiled. *Jennuh*.

The Wyld Louie's Exploding Bear Experience security team walked out the front gate to confront the protesters. Jimmy led the way. Larry and Harry were his wing men. Wyld Louie hung back a safe distance behind them.

Jimmy approached a protester at the front of the group. He was holding a sign that read, DON'T BLOW UP BEARS, JUST BLOW 'EM. The sign was ornate with glitter and sequin patterns. The protester had put a great deal of effort into the sign. The passion for their statement was evident.

"You're monsters! Stop the carnage!" the protester yelled in Jimmy's face.

"Whoa, whoa, whoa," Jimmy said, trying his best to deescalate the situation, "what's with all the hate?"

"You blew up a bear!"

"*Yeah*," the protestors yelled in unison, then quieted down, awaiting an official statement from a representative of Wyld Louie's Exploding Bear Experience.

"Well, yeah. That's what we do here. We've been doing exploding bear experiences for a long time now."

"You can't just blow up our bears!"

Jimmy shook his head. "They're not your bears. We found them, fair and square."

"It's illegal!"

"*Yeah*," the crowd roared.

"It's not illegal. Not in this jurisdiction. Wyld Louie's works under an exemption in the law that has been on the books since the 1600s. It harkens back to a time when wild, saber-toothed bears ravaged the plains. They mauled everything in sight, men, women, *and* especially children. The 1600s Blow Up 'Dem 'Dere Bears Act was signed into law by the late, great Ernest Montgomery

Philbert Aloysius Bernard XIV. No doubt, you've heard of him. Ole Ursine Earl, they called him.

The protestor looked confused. "Ole Ursine Earl? But you said his name was Ernest Montgomery Philbert Aloysius Bernard."

"The fourteenth," Jimmy added.

"There's no Earl in his name."

"Don't disrespect the dead! He was a great statesman! The best, in fact. Read your history, good sir."

Jimmy figured that was the end of that argument. Can't argue with history. What's done is done and the law is the law. Besides, who argues with a guy with a bear arm?

"But our bears aren't ursine," the protestor countered.

Jimmy cursed. This was about the bear that wasn't a bear. He knew blowing up *that* bear would bite them in the ass. Who knew that one bear would bring on a horde of protestors, though?

Jimmy went into damage control. "Wyld Louie is an industry leader. He vets all of his bears to be sure they are ursine. I can assure you, the bear in question here was put through a rigorous, sixteen-point inspection to assure his bear-hood. I can personally assure you, he was asked repeatedly if he was a bear and he insisted, without hesitation, that he was indeed a bear. He was very proud of being a bear, in fact"

The crowd cheered.

Wyld Louie was getting pissed off listening to all the nonsense. He had run a good, clean operation, beloved by many, for a great many years. How dare this unruly mob suggest he was blowing up anything other than bears?

Wyld Louie stepped forward. He'd lick every ass holding up a sign if he had to. It was time to teach them all a lesson they wouldn't soon forget. "Jimmuh! Pick me up, Jimmuh!"

Jimmy lifted Wyld Louie off the ground with his bear arm. Wyld Louie stood perched on Jimmy's massive bear paw, overlooking the protestors. "People! Welcome to Wyld Louie's Exploding Bear Experience. You are all welcome to enjoy a demonstration. If you're not here to witness nature's wonder and majesty happen right in front of your very eyes, then you can just skedaddle! Make way for the paying customers, you ungrateful bastards!"

Jimmy wiped his human hand down his face. Of course Wyld Louie was going to enrage this group instead of placating them. Things were about to get ugly.

And they did when Wyld Louie spotted a PETA sign among the throng.

"Ahh, damn it! This is one of them there Peetuh rallies. Don't you have jobs to go to?"

"We're not PETA we're LGBTQ."

"L-G-B-T what? How am I supposed to say *that*? Lug-guh-buh-tuh-qwah? That isn't even a word!"

"It's not a word, it's an abbreviation."

"Damnit, abbreviations are supposed to make nonsense words that make sense."

"No, you're thinking of acronyms, not abbreviations."

"No, I'm thinking when you form a group like that, you need to come up with a name that makes something that sounds like a word when you string all the letters together. Like Peetuh. You can say that word, even though it's fucked up."

"You're not supposed to say LGBTQ as a word. You just say it as the letters of the words it stands for. That's it."

"What the hell does it even stand for, anyway? Let Go of the Bears That Quickly-blowup?"

The protestor scrunched up his face. "What? No. Have you been living under a rock? It stands for Lesbian, Gay, Bi, Trans and Queer."

"Trans and queer?" Wyld Louie asked. "The hell does trans and queer got to do with bears? You sure the B don't stand for Bears?"

The protestor thought about it for a moment. "I guess, technically it could. But then, what about the bisexuals, how would they be represented?"

"The bisexual bears?"

"All the bisexuals, not just the bears. We probably shouldn't single out the bears in the name, seeing as a bear can be any color of the rainbow."

"I blow up black bears more than anything. That's still a color, even if it's not in the rainbow."

"Listen, Wyld Louie, it's great that you're being inclusive like that, but you still can't blow up our bears. It's unethical and homophobic."

"Homophobic? How the hell is blowing up bears homophobic? You saying I'm blowing up gay bears? That's what this is all about?"

"Yeah! That's why we're here, to stop you from blowing up our bears. It needs to end."

Wyld Louie had had enough. Now, lessons needed to be taught.

"Put me down, Jimmuh," the boss man said. Jimmy eased Wyld Louie back to Earth.

Wyld Louie got right in the protestor's face. "Didn't your mama teach you any manners? I'm an honest man, running an honest shop, doing honest work. I ought to lick your ass like your papa should have done to you years ago."

The protestor presented his rear end to Wyld Louie. His ass was ready to be licked. He was wearing pink leather and assless pants. One of his ass cheeks was tattooed with a tiny little bear face with the word 'cub' underneath.

"Go on," the protestor said, bending at the waist, "teach me something, you big, burly, bear of a man."

Wyld Louie went at the protester's ass faster than he could shove a double explosive up a polar bear's ass. It was one thing when he corrected one of his employees' behaviors, but he went at the protestor's bum with a heightened sense of purpose. This man meant to disrupt his livelihood. That wasn't acceptable. This tongue lashing would have to be stern and forceful.

By the sound of things, Wyld Louie was sending a stern message to his would-be detractor. The protestor was grunting, growling and yelping. It was like he hadn't known what he had coming to him. Wyld Louie was sure this man was being taught like he'd never been taught before.

When it was all over, Wyld Louie stood up and wiped his arm across his mouth. "That's it, boy. You've had enough."

The protestor continued to hold his position and said, "Not nearly."

"What?" Wyld Louie snapped. "How dare you back talk me?! I guess you haven't had enough, after all."

Wyld Louie dove back into the protestor's ass crack. His tongue lashed out at him with unbridled fury.

"Oh yah, that's it, daddy, teach me a lesson. I'm so bad. So, so very, very bad. Ho, yeah! That's it, that's the lesson," the protestor moaned, grabbing an ass cheek and pulling it open for Wyld Louie to really hammer home his point. "I'm learning! I'm learning! Ohhhh!"

Jimmy, Larry and Harry averted their eyes, variously looking up at the sky or down at their toes. They were embarrassed for Wyld Louie, who was definitely missing the point. The protestors were winning. The one being 'taught a lesson' certainly was.

The protestor collapsed to the ground, leaving Wyld Louie's tongue wagging around in the open air for a moment.

The entire mob fell silent.

Another protestor stepped over and presented his posterior to Wyld Louie. "I need to be taught a lesson, too!"

Wyld Louie sighed. He scanned the crowd. It seemed they all felt sorry for what they'd done. Their faces showed they were eager to take their punishments like men. He was going to have his work cut out for him, but he was willing to put in the work if it meant putting an end to these protests.

Wyld Louie went to work on the next protestor.

Jenny watched out the window as Wyld Louie licked well over fifty men's asses. Men, who, unlike Jenny, had zero emotional attachment to the man she loved. And yet, each and every one of them got their asses licked like she'd never seen Wyld Louie tongue a man's ass before.

Jenny sighed. This had to end. It broke her heart.

Chapter 18

The protest turned into a big, steaming pile of satisfaction.

Wyld Louie said, "Naw, ledth th'd buh uh lthhin."

What he tried to say was, *now, let that be a lesson*, but his tongue was numb, dry, and swollen. He'd never given that many punishments at the same time. It wasn't easy, but there are battles worth fighting. This was a war and he won it.

The first protestor that Wyld Louie engaged with had caught his breath after the wildest rumpus he'd ever taken part in. The last thing he expected when he showed up to protest the violence which Wyld Louie was treating the bear community to, was to be left a gelatinous ball of goo by the very man with whom he and his fellow bear lovers took umbrage. But there was no denying that Wyld Louie was a rather persuasive foe.

"I need a cigarette," the protestor sighed.

Jenny brought Wyld Louie a glass of water. She hated him and loved him at the same time. She was red with rage, green with envy and blue with lust after having watched her man tear tongue through a throng of hate-fueled animal rights protestors with a proclivity for fat, hairy men.

"It's almost time for the final demonstration of the day, my love," Jenny said to Wyld Louie.

The words jumped out of her mouth before she could check them. *My love.* They felt natural, despite that fact she felt like she'd just strung a sentence of curse words together like she was some sort of third world sailor who'd made port in a second-rate country.

Wyld Louie looked dazed, like he was punch drunk after going twelve rounds with Mike Tyson. There was so much information for his brain to process in that small moment: the next demonstration, was there a bear ready, what was he going to do with the heap of protestors who'd had their attitudes put in check and what the hell with that 'my love' talk? Wyld Louie didn't know which burning question he needed an answer to first. He couldn't ask any of them outright because his tongue was swollen five times its normal size. He was a total mush mouth.

Jimmy, ever the faithful employee and master bear wrangler, saw Wyld Louie's struggle and rose to the occasion. "I'll get the bear ready, don't you worry. Harry, go get the animals ready in the petting zoo. Larry, fire up the grills and pick up all the animal crap lying around. We're about to have a big rush, right here, at the end of the day.

Jimmy addressed the protestors, "Can I have your attention please? As an act of goodwill and a show of good faith for the progress we've made here today, Wyld

Louie would like to invite you all in to witness the final demonstration of the day, free of charge!"

The protestors jumped to their feet and laid down their signs.

Wyld Louie clutched his chest. Free of charge? "Jennuh! Jennuh! Help me, I think I'm having a heart attack!"

Jenny fell to her knees at Wyld Louie's side. She wouldn't let him die. Not today. She straddled him and began mouth to mouth resuscitation. It wasn't necessary but it saved his life, nonetheless.

As Jenny pounded away at Wyld Louie's chest, one of the protestors put his hand on her shoulder. "You're going to have to lick his ass. It's the only way."

Jenny was stunned. Of course. It was obvious. The tongue baths to the rectum breathed new life into everyone who basked in the sensation. That's why Louie dished out punishments left and right, everyone corrected their bad behavior when he was done with them. He even turned an unruly mob to his way of thinking by lapping at their assholes like a kitten working over a warm bowl of milk.

Jenny rolled Wyld Louie over and tugged down his trousers.

She gazed at his butt cheeks, two bulbous, hairy, dingleberry encrusted ass cheeks. She could never love another set of buns more than her dear, sweet Wyld Louie's pock ridden, dimpled ass cheeks, peppered with red boils where the crack cast a shadow into the crevice of his nether region. She split him apart like she was tearing open an over ripened peach. The scent she was greeted with smelled like a rotten peach, too.

With the fever of Indiana Jones, on a quest for another bad installment of his movie franchise, she dove in, tongue first.

Wyld Louie gasped and breathed the way bad actors start breathing again after fake drowning in a cartoonish sit-com. "Gahhhhh!" he croaked, then moaned because he was getting his asshole licked by the woman who cared for him most. Which was good, because that's exactly what was happening at that moment.

Wyld Louie felt revived. Refreshed. Invigorated. And... charitable. The thought of allowing hundreds of free admissions to his exploding bear experience seemed more wholesome. He allowed Jenny to finish, then he stood up.

Wyld Louie felt like he had discovered the trigger for lasting world peace.

All he was saying was, give ass licking a chance.

"I love you, Jennuh," Wyld Louie said.

Jenny jumped into his arms, and they made out while the former protestors entered the park in an orderly fashion, becoming welcomed guests.

Chapter 19

Jenny crunched the numbers. Things didn't look good. Wyld Louie's had been eking by the past few months. No matter how frugal Wyld Louie ran the operation, it still wasn't enough.

Worse yet, Wyld Louie had no idea how dire the situation had become. He figured they were rolling in dough after the bork burgers started selling well. He saw the steady stream of income the adhesive sales were bringing in, and he knew damn well he wasn't paying his employees diddly squat. They were doing well working for tips at the petting zoo.

Jenny didn't know how to break it to Wyld Louie. She couldn't crush his spirits. She'd come so far with him today. If she was the bearer of bad news, it would crush the progress she'd made.

Jenny needed to step up as office manager and figure this out herself.

But, how could they squeeze more money out of the guests? Admissions, food, and souvenirs; what more was there to take? There had to be an angle they hadn't considered yet.

Jenny rapped her fingers on the desk, running ideas through her mind. What were other entertainment parks doing to make money? They could bring in carnival rides. There are always old, broken down, rust-bucket rides for sale from the carnie circuit. Problem is, there really wasn't enough land to set up any rides. They'd have to buy up more forest land around the park, but then they'd lose bear habitat. Wyld Louie would never make that trade-off.

They could do bear rides. That might work. Sell tickets to ride a bear right before it exploded. There was a thrill factor there. They could rig up a saddle with a ticking clock that would really scare the shit out of the guests. Of course, there was a high risk of guests getting mauled if the bear wasn't properly tranquilized. Jimmy had been having a hell of a time sourcing bears lately. There wasn't a whole lot of time to set up bear rides ahead of blowing them up. So, that idea was out.

Wyld Louie stomped into the office. Jenny stood straight up and tightened her expression into a business professional blank face. It was a natural reaction when Wyld Louie entered a room. Within moments he would spew vitriol about whatever problem-du-jour he was irate with at the Exploding Bear Experience. But Jenny spied Wyld Louie out of the corner of her eye and found he was beaming from ear to ear.

She relaxed.

"Yeah, Jennuh! I feel so alive!" Wyld Louie announced, like he was a used car salesman in a local cable channel commercial.

"That's because I saved your life," Jenny said, then paused and added, "baby."

Wyld Louie's smile was big and genuine. It was aimed right at Jenny. "Babuh, huh?" Wyld Louie skidded to one knee in front of Jenny. "Jennuh, will you marruh me, babuh?"

Jenny swooned. Her legs went numb and she almost collapsed to the floor. Had Wyld Louie just proposed marriage to her? Could it be true? Did he actually ask if she would marry him? "Marruh you?" Jenny asked.

From down on one knee, Wyld Louie's face went beet red. "Damnit, Jennuh! I said marruh, not marruh! I'm done being nice to you, babuh." Wyld Louie spun Jenny around by the hips and yanked down her yoga pants. "Now you listen, and you listen good."

Wyld Louie buried his tongue in Jenny's asshole like he was the plumber, and her anus was clogged with seventeen years of yeti hair build up. Jenny yelped the way porn actresses do when they're overpaid and double teamed.

Jenny was in heaven. "Yes! Wyld Louie! I'll marruh you! I'll marruh you every day and I won't ever say marruh the way you want me to say marruh and you'll teach me a lesson every blessed day for the rest of our lives."

Jenny came.

Wyld Louie pulled her pants back up, satisfied she'd learned her lesson today and content knowing she wanted to be taught every day from here 'til death do they part.

Jenny crumpled into Wyld Louie's arms. An idea struck her the way the orgasm had hit her, hard. "Let's get married here. At the Exploding Bear Experience. We can build a wedding pavilion. We'll be the very first couple to get married here. And, you know how at Jewish weddings they stomp on a fancy glass wrapped in a napkin and it makes a loud pop? We can do that with a bear! Wrap it in a napkin and you stomp on it, and it'll explode for good luck! Oh yes! Yes! I'll marry you, Wyld Louie! I'll get started on the wedding pavilion project right away! This'll get us out of the red for sure!"

Jenny dashed to her desk and began tapping on her keyboard in a whirlwind.

"Did you say, 'out of the red', Jennuh? Are we broke?"

Jenny forgot she wasn't supposed to say anything. There went the marriage and the wedding pavilion with it. "Yes," she admitted, like a girl caught doing something she ought not do.

"Okay. No problem. I have the perfect solution. You just keep planning that wedding pavilion and our nuptials. I've got to find Jimmuh, and a camera. We've got some promoting to do before we open tomorrow."

Chapter 20

A man named Drew turned on his television. As usual, there wasn't shit on worth watching. Drew scanned the channel guide.

Bullshit.

Bullshit.

Bullshit.

Oh! FailArmy. You could never go wrong putting on the FailArmy channel. It's a twenty-four-hour marathon of people getting fucked up almost to the edge of death. Mostly dudes getting their nards hammered harder than humanly possible. One time, Drew caught a clip of a guy getting crotch charged by a rhinoceros when he wandered into its enclosure at the zoo, like the drunken idiot he was. Though the scene cut to the next bozo getting his junk pounded, Drew was certain that dude was walking around with an innie dong to this very day.

Of course, as soon as he tuned into FailArmy, there was a commercial. FailArmy was really just a YouTube feed, but since it was on cable, the cable company ran local commercial ads every so often. Ya know, to fatten their pockets a little more.

Under normal circumstances that would have been enough for Drew to continue on to another channel of mindless entertainment. But something about the commercial, that began running the moment Drew flipped to the channel, grabbed him by the collar and demanded his attention.

On the screen, a bear exploded.

Bear guts and gore washed the camera lens. The bear's eyeball slithered down the screen for a moment before it cut to the image of a man wearing a white suit and a white cowboy hat, standing on a deck, overlooking a picturesque cliffside.

"Hey, friends! Wyld Louie here, inviting you all down to Wyld Louie's Exploding Bear Experience for our big ole Exploding Bear-O-Rama!"

The commercial cut to a shot of two bears standing in front of the cliffside Wyld Louie was standing in front of. *Kaboom!* The two bears exploded at the same time. Drew's TV screen filled with the resulting massacre once more. Drew even flinched backward on his couch and tossed his remote from the unexpected explode-scare.

The shot cut back to Wyld Louie. His pristine white uniform was covered in running rivers of blood. His hat remained pure as the driven snow. "Woo dogguh! And that was just two bears! C'mon down to Wyld Louie's Exploding Bear Experience tomorrow to experience the all-new Exploding Bear-O-Rama, where you'll experience not one... not two... but... well, we're going to load up our exploding bear exhibit with as many dang exploding bears as we can cram in there. And then we're going to blow them all to kingdom come! Ain't that right, Jimmuh?"

The scene cut to a man, in frame from the waist up, and one of his arms was a bear's arm. "That's right, Wyld Louuh," said Jimmy. Then Jimmy took a swipe at the camera with his bear arm, for effect. But the movement was mechanical, forced, and fit right in with the amateur late-night cable commercial motif.

From off-camera you could hear Wyld Louie say, "Damnit, Jimmuh! My name's not Louuh, it's Louuh! Why I ought to rip down your dang trousers and lick your—"

Jimmy, still in the shot, whispered out of the side of his mouth, "We're recording, sir." He was confident his ventriloquist skills were above par and the audience watching at home wouldn't pick up the exchange.

The camera cut back to Wyld Louie, who smoothed down his jacket and said, "Right, right." He cleared his throat and continued his pitch, "Get here early, folks! You're going to want to get a good spot for this unique experience featuring Wyld Louie's one-of-a-kind exploding bear experience.

"Don't bother eating because we've got the best bork burgers this side of the Mississippi. Hell, we've got the best bork burgers on the other side of the Mississippi too! And don't worry, if you get impaled with exploding bear bits and pieces, your Uncle Wyld Louie has got you covered. We sell the best varnishes, lacquers, and three-part epoxies that money can buy, so you can shellac those bad boys to your body and save them for a lifetime of posterity. Or 8 to 12 weeks, whichever comes first."

Oh shit! Drew was on his phone texting everyone he knew. He wouldn't miss Wyld Louie's Exploding Bear-O-

Rama for the world. He shot a group text to Alicia, Rayne, Simon, Sean, Lucy, Matt, Lucas, John, Peter, Lewis, Jason, Nick, Daniel, Tom, Marian, Mort, Christina, and those five idiots from New Jersey.

"Yo! Tomorrow. Wyld Louie's. He's blowin' up all the bears. Gonna be rad. Be there. 8am. We're getting front row seats. You better be there 2"

Chapter 21

Jimmy cleared the forest of every living bear. It was ridiculous how easy it was to wrangle bears when you had a bear arm and a human mind. Jimmy pulled in five black bears, two browns, and a sun bear that got lost on its way to Bangkok. If the sun bear blew up in just the right way, some lucky patron was going to get an extra-long tongue shellacked to their face. What a treat!

Jimmy even picked up a polar bear when the winds blew in out of the north and the giant white ursine beast wandered into Jimmy's bear arm like it was an igloo full of tasty Innuits. To top it all off, Wyld Louie's new LGBTQ+ advisor, Gary, stepped up to the plate and provided Jimmy with a small glass vial full of bears.

"What is it, Garuh?" Wyld Louie asked.

"It's a test tube full of water bears. Oh, and it's Gary, not Garuh," Gary said.

"Damnit, Garuh! I said Garuh, not Garuh. Clean out your dang ears, boy!" Wyld Louie said.

"Aren't you going to lick my ass and teach me a lesson?"

"Damnit, Garuh! We don't have time for that right now," Wyld Louie said.

"I don't see any bears in this vial," Larry said, holding the vial up to the bridge of his nose.

"Oh, they're in there. Water bears are microscopic. Fancy people call them tardigrades. They're so fucking cute!" Gary said.

"Damnit, Garuh, I know a water bear when I see one. They're all big and blubbery and walk around on sticks for legs and they've got a unicorn horn on their head. We blew one up here not too long ago."

Gary scratched his head and said, "That sounds more like a narwhal with two-by-fours strapped to his body than it does a tardigrade."

"Either way, how in the hell am I going to load a charge into a microscopic bear, Garuh?"

Gary looked confused. He hadn't thought it through that far. He just figured bears exploded here at Wyld Louie's. He was a bit taken aback to find out the explosions were rigged. "You could, uhh, shove them up another exploding bear's ass and just let them blow up with it, I guess."

Wyld Louie slapped Gary on the back. "That's a brilliant idea, Garuh!"

"Gary," Gary corrected, not missing an opportunity to be corrected once again.

"Keep it up, Garuh," Wyld Louie said, pointing a finger at Gary but then slapping him on the back once more.

"Oh, I will sir. I will."

"Jimmuh, cram those water bears up that grizzly's ass. Make sure we let everyone know we blew up some water bears too. Hell, I might be able to sell extra glue if I convince some of these people they've got microscopic bear parts embedded in them."

Wyld Louie was ecstatic! Nothing was going to break his stride.

Jenny entered the office. She wore a pristine white dress with a long train that followed in her wake, which was embroidered with teddy bear faces. "I'm ready to be married," she said.

Wyld Louie's stride was broken.

"Damnit, Jennuh!" Wyld Louie said, "I'm not ready to be marruh'd"

Jimmy shoved Wyld Louie into his office. "Whoa! Mustn't let the groom see the bride in her dress," he said to Jenny as he slammed the door behind them. "What do you mean you're not ready to get married? This is it. This is the big day. You know how much work went into this. You know how much the future of the park hinges on you and Jenny getting married. Damnit, Wyld Louie, sir, I can't face a day in the real world. I *need* this place. We all need this place. It's the only situation where the world makes sense. If I ain't the guy with the bear arm that blows up bears, what am I?"

Wyld Louie was floored. Wyld Louie's Exploding Bear Experience had always been his business. It was his thing. He'd started this place with a dollar and a dream. He'd made it something bigger than himself. It wasn't about the bears and the customers and his bank account. Wyld Louie's Exploding Bear Experience was bigger than Wyld Louie, now. Wyld Louie wasn't a name, it was a family. A family of misfits, miscreants, and mammals. Jimmuh was right, he had to marry Jennuh. He was having a case of nerves, but everyone was depending on him. In a way, they were all getting married today.

"Alright, your right, Jimmuh," Wyld Louie said, gripping Jimmy's shoulder. "You're right. I just got a case of nerves, is all. I mean, one woman, for the rest of my life. That's big."

"But, what a woman. Jenny is a great catch. She's perfect for you. You're perfect for her."

"You side eyeing' my wife, Jimmuh? Do I have to pull down your pants and put you in your place before I take my bride-to-be, Jimmuh? Damnit, Jimmuh, I'm not a cuck!"

Jimmy smiled and said, "No, sir. You don't need to pull down my pants. You're not a cuck."

"That's more like it. Okay, tell Jennuh I'm ready. Let's get this show on the road."

Jimmy opened the office door and peeked out. "He's ready. Let's do this."

The observation platform at Wyld Louie's Exploding Bear Experience was packed with as many guests as the fire marshal would allow (at least, that's what they told the fire marshal.) A makeshift altar was placed along the railing overlooking the exploding bear enclosure.

The wedding party began their march down the aisle to the sultry sounds of the melodic opera group, iwrestledabearonce. The party was led by Jimmy, who served as the officiant of the ceremony. Jimmy was followed by a shaved porcupine with strawberry jelly smeared on its asshole. The de facto beaver from the petting zoo was the ring bearer, it had a red velvet pillow duct-taped to its back. Harry hoped its esteemed status in the wedding party would garner bigger tips from customers who wanted to lick its ass after the ceremony. And that was pretty much it for the wedding party.

Jenny walked down the aisle to a piece from William Walton's opera, 'The Bear.' Wyld Louie held back a tear. Jenny looked so beautiful. So beautiful, in fact, that he should lick her ass for being too pretty. She was the perfect bride, on a perfect day, in the most perfect place on Earth.

Jenny took her place next to Wyld Louie at the altar as a brown bear exploded behind them, showering the couple in viscera.

Jimmy, wearing vestments made of bear hide, began the ceremony. "Dearly beloved, we have gathered here today, at Wyld Louie's Exploding Bear Experience, where gift certificates are available in the gift shop."

The guests oohed softly. Everyone was a sucker for a subtle pitch during a serious moment.

Jimmy continued, "To join this woman and this man, the man who discovered the first exploding bear twenty years ago as he trekked the wilds of the north-central Alaskan tundra of the south. It was there that a humble man named Louis Wooie, was named Wyld Louie when he wrestled an exploding bear and brought it back to the mainland to demonstrate their natural powers to the masses."

"Your name is Louie Wooie?" Jenny interrupted.

"Jennuh, just call me Wyld Louuh, don't worry about any of that."

"But my name is going to be Mrs. Louie Wooie," Jenny said. Hearing it out loud made it sound even worse.

"Damnit, Jennuh, you're going to be Jennuh and that's all."

Wyld Louie, an expert at damage control, did his best spin doctoring. "Jennuh, babuh, right before the ceremony, I changed my legal name to Louuh Louuh. Like the song! See? So, you're going to be Mrs. Wyld Louuh Louuh."

Jenny tilted her head like a curious puppy. "Mrs. Louie Louie. I like that. I like that a lot." She turned to Jimmy and said, "Okay, go on."

Jimmy proceeded through all the formalities of the marriage ceremony with appropriate pomp and circumstance. He was a natural officiant. Before long, he got to the part that everyone was waiting for. "Do you, Wyld Louie Woo... err, Wyld Louie Louie, take this woman, Jennifer Ursine Brown, to be your lawfully wedded wife?"

A bead of sweat appeared on the ridge of Wyld Louie's brow, but he had his loving gaze locked on his bride-to-be and powered through the all-important moment. "I do."

"And do you, Jennifer Ursine Brown, take this man, Wyld Louie Louie, to be your lawfully wedded husband? To have and to hold, to love and to squeeze, like your giant teddy bear, for as long as you both shall live?"

Wyld Louie glared at Jimmy. "Damnit, Jimmuh! What the hell is all that nonsense?"

Jenny put her hand on Wyld Louie's cheek and coxed his gaze back to her. "It's okay, baby, I told him to add that bit. To stay on brand, you know?" she asked with a wink.

So help him, Wyld Louie could have sworn that her eyes twinkled and a bell from the Heavens chimed as she winked. "Okay, okay. Go on, Jimmuh, let's bring this home. We got bears to blow up."

"You still have to say, I do," Jimmy reminded Wyld Louie.

"I do! I really, really do!"

"Then, with the power vested in me by the Western Northeast Collective of Non-Denominational Ministers of the Southern Areas, I now pronounce you husband and wife. You may now kiss your wild bride."

Wyld Louie went in for a peck. Jenny took her newly crowned husband with the full length of her tongue. The crowd gasped at first but warmed up to the over-exaggerated expression of love taking place right in front of them.

Soon, the warm vibes changed to uncomfortable silence as Wyld Louie, overwhelmed by the emotion of the moment, crawled up into Jenny's white wedding dress where, one would assume, he began to teach her her first lesson as his wife. Her spirited moans left little room to argue otherwise.

Jimmy, at first captivated by the raw display of pure human emotion, broke free of the spell, retrieved a party popper tangled up in his furry bear arm, aimed it to the sky, and said, "Ladies, gentlemen, and bears alike, it is my honor to present, for the first time, Mr. and Mrs. Wyld Louie Louie!"

The congregation erupted in applause.

Wyld Louie jumped out from under Jenny's dress. She collapsed, spent. "Don't forget, Wyld Louie's Exploding Bear Wedding Pavilion Experience is now available, year 'round, to all you lovely couples out there. We offer the venue, an officiant, open bar, and catered reception, featuring our world-famous Borkinator Burger Bar, live music compliments of our house band, The Petting Zoo, and of course, one complimentary exploding bear. It's a one-of-a-kind wedding ceremony that cannot be duplicated, by law, anywhere else in these United States, its territories, and all English-speaking nations.

Now, as promised, to celebrate our marriage and to kick off the grand opening of Wyld Louie's Exploding Bear Wedding Pavilion Experience, please gather around the observation platform and enjoy this rare exploding bear experience, Wyld Louie's Exploding Bear-O-Rama!"

The Petting Zoo, a ragtag band, formed just that morning when Wyld Louie sent Jimmy to the pawnshop to buy as many used instruments as they had in stock, broke into a terrible rendition of 'Disco Inferno.' It was the only fire-branded song they could find a beginner's level tutorial for on YouTube.

To Harry's credit, his kazoo playing transcended the abilities of the rest of the band. The drummer, Larry, used a cracked bucket from the pawn shop (yes, Jimmy bought a cracked bucket from the pawnshop.) The bass was a used Rickenbacker with the headstock busted off and only two strings that were held in place with duct tape. Barry joked and said it wasn't a wedding band, it was a jug band. He fetched the old plastic milk jug he used to pee in when the bathrooms were overrun and too nasty to use. He blew into it and gave The Petting Zoo their backbeat.

Chapter 22

The reception was grand. The guests danced to renditions of 'Disco Inferno,' 'The Electric Slide,' 'The Macarena,' and 'Runaround Sue,' played by The Petting Zoo. There was a fine catered meal of pizza and Borkinator burgers. After everyone ate, and just before cake and coffee, it was time for the big show. Wyld Louie stood at a podium to the side of the observation deck as his wedding guests crammed in around the railing.

"It's time for Wyld Louie's Exploding Bear-O-Rama!" he announced to a round of raucous applause.

A brown bear with a glass jar crammed up its ass walked out on the platform. Jenny stood against the railing with her back to the bear and tossed her bouquet over into the enclosure. The gorgeous bundle of flowers landed in front of the bear. The bear took a sniff test to see if it was a food source. As his adorable bear tongue lapped at the bouquet, *BLAM!*

The bear exploded.

The crowd oohed and ahhed as pieces of bear jetted into the throng of onlookers.

"Oh, Harold, I've got a shard of glass in my arm," a woman cried out.

Wyld Louie, from his podium, announced, "Oh, and what a lucky lady you are to have been impaled with the very first exploding water bears! Larry, get that lady some shellac!"

Larry raced over to the woman, bucket of shellac and brush at the ready. Without hesitation, Larry encased the shard of glass in the woman's arm with a thick coating. "Let that set for ten minutes before swimming. We'll bill that to your Wyld Louie's Exploding Bear Experience account." Larry produced an RFID scanner and scanned a wristband the woman wore.

Every guest at Wyld Louie and Jenny's wedding received one. Everyone who entered the park from here on out would receive one. They attached a credit card to their ticket, and bam, Wyld Louie was able to charge guests for a plethora of junk he previously would have had to beg them to pony up the cash for. It was too easy.

Wyld Louie had his wife, Jenny, to thank for that innovation. He cursed himself for not letting her manage the business sooner. Between the wedding pavilion and the new credit card wristbands, the park was already back in the black.

Two grizzly bears and a panda bear walked out into the enclosure. *BLAM! BLAM-BLAM!* All three exploded like fireworks. Bone and gristle whizzed into the crowd. More onlookers were impaled. Larry painted on shellac and scanned wrist bands at a furious pace.

The next set of bears came out. A polar bear, five black bears and a grizzly-looking man. It was Bear Grylls, the celebrity television survivalist.

"No fuckin' way," one guy said when he noticed the celebrity bear.

"Bear Grylls! Wooo!" another young man called out.

Bear Grylls looked stoned, like all the other bears he was grouped with. There was a red stick protruding from his ass. It sparkled like the Fourth of July.

KA-BLAM!

Bear Grylls, and all his bear friends, exploded. He didn't survive.

Larry shellacked Bear Grylls' finger to the guy who first noticed him and scanned his wristband. He moved on to attend to the others who were impaled with less famous parts of less famous bears. There was money to be made, no time to dwell on celebrity.

A Kodiak bear wondered into the explosion zone, followed by all the surviving members of the Chicago Bears who had won the 1986 Super Bowl. William "The Refrigerator" Perry was bigger than the Kodiak.

Someone in the crowd yelled, "The 'Fridge!" before all the bears went, *WA-PLAM!*

One of the guest's left eye was replaced with the jewel of William Perry's championship ring. Larry shellacked it in place. The shellac stung the guest's eye and would later cause him to go blind, but Larry scanned his wristband, nonetheless.

A fuzzy orange bear, a bulbous panda bear, and a giant purple bear all walked out, standing upright. The smell of strawberries filled the air.

"Ohh," said a young boy whose face looked like he just walked into a sweet shop. "It's Lotso Huggin' Bear!"

The boy's mother laughed. "And Fozzy Bear, too!"

"And that panda from, what's that movie?" the father asked.

"Kung-Fu Panda," the boy said.

Pa-POW!

The cartoon bear trio exploded. Larry glued Fozzy Bear's hat to a patron and scanned his wristband. Harry was on his hands and knees, franticly looking for Lotso Huggin' Bear's anus. If he smelled like strawberries, his ass was sure to be worth licking. He could make bank charging visitors to lap at Lotso's disembodied anus.

Wyld Louie called out, "Are there any more bears back there we haven't exploded yet?"

Jimmy coughed and said, "Actually, Wyld Louie, sir, the boys and I put together a little finale you didn't know about as a sort of wedding gift to you and Jenny."

Jenny tilted her head and mouthed an adorable, "aww, so sweet."

Wyld Louie had a different but very Wyld Louie reaction. "What? Unapproved bear explosion? Damnit, Jimmuh, I should pull down all your britches and teach you and the boys a lesson you won't soon forget."

Jenny tugged her husband's chin in her direction. "Uh-uh. The only one you'll be teaching a lesson to from here on out is me, my little exploding sugar-bear-bugga-boo."

Wyld Louie blushed. "Oh, alright."

A koala bear trotted into the enclosure. He was full of vim and vigor. Unusual for an exploding bear, as they're usually tranquilized. Wyld Louie watched in horror, Larry and the others had broken strict protocol. Plus, Wyld Louie didn't see the tell-tale sparkles from a lit charge burning out of the koala's asshole. He just might have to sneak in a lesson to Jimmuh and the others for this level of insubordination.

The crowd clamored closer to the railing, super intrigued by the cute koala. Someone in the crowd stated the obvious, "But, koala bears aren't bears. They're marsupials."

Wyld Louie was annoyed by the interruption of his wedding gift. "Damnit, person! It's a koala bear. Bear. Says so right in the name. Stop being such an idiot and shut up and enjoy my gift."

As the koala reached the center of the demonstration area, from out of thin air, another bear, a tad bigger than the koala, but with orange fur and leopard spots, fell from the sky and landed on top of the normal looking koala.

"Holy shit!" someone in the crowd said, recognizing the bear that seemed to have dropped in without a parachute.

"Well, I'll be a shit-slingin', acid-spittin', dung-flingin', stank-bringin', swill-lickin', pud-poundin', ass-grabbin' monkey's uncle. That is a genuine Australian Drop Bear. The Holy Fuckin' Grail."

KA-BOOM!

The Australian Drop Bear exploded and took out the koala with it. It was the most magnificent thing Wyld Louie had ever witnessed in his entire life. A tear of joy rolled down his cheek. Then, a tear of joy rolled down Jenny's cheek when she witnessed her husband have a raw moment of happiness for the first time in his life.

"Thank you, Jimmuh. Thank you, everyone. That was spectacular."

Wyld Louie lifted Jenny off her feet. He carried her off the observation deck and into his office. The crowd applauded them the whole way.

There, in the offices of Wyld Louie's Exploding Bear Experience and Wedding Pavilion, Wyld Louie and Jenny Louie consummated their marriage.

There were more weddings. A lot more weddings. There were more exploding bears. A lot more exploding bears. The new business model was an incredible success. They even secured a genuine beaver with a strawberry flavored ass in the petting zoo, thus reducing the risk of further legal action.

They never blew up another Australian Drop Bear again.

KABOOM!

THE END

Other Books by Frank J. Edler

Death Gets a Book

Brats in Hell

Scatterbrain

Catcoin: The Fictional History of a Cryptocurrency

A Death in Toledo

Scared Silly

Uncomfortable Shorts

With Armand Rosamilia

Shocker

Shocker II: Love Gun

Shocker III: Slippery When Wet

With Chuck Buda, Tim Meyer and Armand Rosamilia

Beers and Fears: The Haunted Brewery

Beers and Fears: Flight Night

Frank J. Edler is the author of *Death Gets a Book*, *Brats In Hell*, *Catcoin*, and more. His writing walks the fine line between horror and the bizarre. He resides in New Jersey, a land that is both horrific and bizarre.

His social media contacts are:

Facebook: www.facebook.com/FrankJEdler

Twitter: @NJMetal

Instagram: NJMetal

Blog: frankjedler.blogspot.com

TIKTOK: MrFrank732

Made in the USA
Middletown, DE
17 October 2023

40753631R10083